WE THE HUNTERS

WE THE HUNTERS

A. ALEX COME'

ARPress
ILLUMINATING IDEAS,
EMPOWERING VOICES

ARPress
45 Dan Road Suite 5
Canton, MA 02021

Hotline: 1(888) 821-0229
Fax: 1(508) 545-7580

Ordering Information:
Quantity sales. Special discounts are available on quantity purchases by corporations, associations, and others. For details, contact the publisher at the address above.

Printed in the United States of America.

ISBN-13:   Softcover   979-8-89330-892-1
                eBook   979-8-89330-893-8

Library of Congress Control Number: 2024902592

TABLE OF CONTENTS

CHAPTER ONE

Hands resting on the saddle-horn, tired eyes drank-in the splendor of the Colorado Mountains. Snow was cascading from a sky of blue while bright rays of sun warmed my face. A soft breeze danced with the sea of snow-capped pine and everywhere a thick blanket of white glittered like a lost sea of diamonds. So spellbinding was it, I'd nearly forgot my purpose for being here.

Thomas Wade was a good man. Almost too good: Lawman, Father, Best Friend and Churchgoer with his family when time permitted. Sadly Of course, that was all history now. As of three days ago he had ceased being my deputy and become a wanted man. So now, I, Arch Steinberge, United States Marshal, had become his Hunter.

Pulling the makings from my coat pocket I rolled a smoke. When lit I inhaled deeply, scanning the northern slopes as best a man can through falling snow.

Tom's tracks had now all but disappeared. Yet, I was certain he was nearby; probably watching me right now. If I were tracking any other man, I'd never sit my horse in this manner, out in the open in the middle of a snow-covered meadow, but for Tom, this was my best chance. I was far from the tree line and if he were to take a shot, although I doubted, he would, chances were he'd miss.

What I really hoped to gain was communication, for Tom to trust in our friendship and call out. Warn me to go home.

Wanting to move, Gertrude snorted shaking her head with warm breath steaming from her nose. She was a good mount, and I patted her neck. Taking one last draw from the cigarette I tossed it down hearing it hiss at the cold white snow. It was time to move.   Reining eastward I headed for the distant slopes. Another two, maybe three hours, and it would be time to make camp. The white powder was deep, and Gertrude labored with each step.

Around us the snow continued to fall steadily. It would be dangerous and equally senseless to keep moving. In the pine forest ahead, I'd find a close group of Spruce and bed down, build a warm fire in a makeshift lean-to and settle in. Coffee, that's what I'd make, strong and hot, fry some bacon, mix it with a chunk of hard tack then lay back and watch the white stuff fall through the night.

Breathing in the fresh mountain air I thought about Tom again. What he was doing I could not blame him for. Any man with a sane mind would do the same. Unfortunately, the law interprets right and wrong based on can and can nots. It was known 3 to 5 men had killed his son and daughter, then burned them all in the house along with his wife. Everyone had shared Tom's grief, but no one knew for sure who had committed the murders, except Tom himself.

Following his suspicions, he beat a confession out of one of them, found out they had raped his wife before killing all three and burning down his home. Tom had learned the remaining four names then began hunting them down sending each to the maker for judgment. However, one had managed to elude Tom. A bad one, cold blooded. This man did not avoid Tom because he was scared; he rode away hard because he was smart, smart like a fox. Granger was a killer who knew just how to play the game and not get caught on the wrong side of the law. Rumor had it even as a baby Granger preferred sucking the barrel of a gun than his mother's tit when hungry. He liked a good game of poker too, but this time he sat at the wrong table and played the wrong card; he beat the law but messed with Tom Wade.

By the time darkness covered the mountains I was well into the slopes and lying inside the lean-to. Bacon was cooking and coffee boiling, it smelled good, and I was hungry. I had banked the fire at the lean-to entrance, and it was warm enough I had removed my heavy coat. Firelight danced on the canvas walls and outside snow continued to fall. The burning wood crackled and snapped amid the flickering flames; it's sound one of my favorites, and along with it, the aroma somehow drew me close to the Maker.

After rolling a smoke I poured a cup of the steaming coffee then leaned back against my saddle thinking, what to do about Tom? He was a good friend, the best I've ever known. Tom had been my deputy for over eight years. We had fought together, tracked side by side for weeks on end, suffered in loss and gloried in gain. We had saved the others life more than once and now because of the very law we both believed in, one might die by the hand of the other.

I set the pan of bacon to one side and plucked out a couple of strips with my knife. Along with the hardtack they went down with tasty satisfaction. Beyond the lean-to it was black as a widow's veil. Yawing, I stretched, and it felt good.

Although tired, sleep would not come for a while. My mind was filled with indecision and my heart lay heavier than a blacksmith's anvil. Being honest with myself, I wondered just what I'd do; really do, when I caught up with Tom?

Would I… could I really lock him in chains? Laying my badge aside I was in full agreement he had every right in doing what he did, and each of those men deserved what he gave them. Besides, even if he had dragged them all into court alive, there was no evidence for conviction; only a forced confession on Tom's part, and every one of them would have marched in with ten witnesses swearing to the judge they were innocent.

Taking a sip of coffee, I shook my head. Why was I even pondering it? The law was the law! Besides, justice always wins in the end isn't that the way we're taught. To be honest, I sometimes wonder if vigilante groups aren't the right law, the true law, the law of nature, eye for an eye. Hell, even all mighty saw it that way, you do wrong, you pay. Simple, so the question is why did we complicate it?

Soberly I stared into my coffee cup and swirled the black contents. Bottom line, plain and simple, my job was to bring Tom in. That's all there was to it.

The cigarette I held had burned down to my fingers, so I tossed it out of the lean-to watching it arched through the darkness and falling snow. Being a U.S. Marshall was not always easy and it seemed the older I got the more black and white things turned into gray. In my heart I hoped Tom was far away and heading for Mexico; and while I openly admit I don't exactly ride tall in the saddle when it comes to religion, I certainly wished him God's speed.

The fire flickered and a piece of the burning wood popped. In my head I said a little prayer for Tom. Then, for what it was worth sent one up for myself; asking the good Lord to see to it that Granger himself crossed my path.

It was a long while and several cups of coffee before sleep came. I woke several times during the night and fed the fire. By the time morning sunshine arrived the sky was clear and the snow had stopped.

Setting the coffee pot over a flame, I stepped out of the lean-to and looked up into a blue sky. Almost a foot of new snow had fallen and glittered bright beneath the sun's glare. For me the chase was over. There would be no trailing Tom now, his tracks were long buried. Inside of me there was emptiness, and a touch of thankfulness too. They say a man must accept his destiny; that what will be will be. They also say you can never go back, and I realized that as truth; it was time to admit Tom Wade was gone.

Back in Denver my office would be waiting with a bottomless pot of coffee on the stove. Turning I crawled back into the lean-to and began packing things up. Out of sight out of mind, that was the way it had to be.

With reluctance my heart told Tom good-by; the way it is, is the way it is. At least, that's what I thought while dumping the remaining coffee on the fire. "It's over," I told the steam rising from the ashes, "he's gone and it's time to go home. I whispered it again, "Time to go home!" Way down deep, amid the emptiness, the words gave me little solace.

*

The slopes on which we climbed were steep and the snow thick. Gertrude struggled harder than she had yesterday. Dismounting I put on snowshoes and pulled her behind. For me the walking was tiring, but on her the snow was belly deep. I felt sorry for her but there was little I could do short of moving slow and easy.

Denver, to my best guess, was another two days travel. However, given I was on course and luck was riding with us, we'd reach Central City by nightfall. There were certainly worse places we could put up for an evening. The place was a crazy, untamed mining town filled with wild men who worked hard and lived the same way. But at least there would be a stable for Gurtrude and the Teller House Hotel for me. The place was expensive, but the city of Denver would pick up the tab; after all, this U.S. Marshall was out on official business.

As the day pushed on the air grew colder and gray clouds buried the sun. The beautiful weather was giving birth to one hell of a storm and the last thing I wanted was to be caught in it. Up here it was easy for a man to lose his way. The trees, distant slopes, and rock formations he used as landmarks were often changed by the snow, making it a dangerous place to be, even for experienced mountain men. And for certain it was no place for haste or panic.

More than once I'd come upon the remains of some lost soul who'd prayed with his last breath a traveler would come along and find him; and often someone had, a pack of starving wolves and vultures.

*

We rode into Central City late. There were six stars in the night sky, a lonely moon and bone freezing wind that had turned the air into a raw, life-threatening killer. Gurtrude wanted a warm place to bed down as much as myself; so, my first stop was the stable. It's said no one grows closer to his horse than a cowboy. Such stories are true, and such is the case between Gurtrude and me. In fact, I had affectionately given her my mother's name. It had brought a belly laugh from many a man, but old Gurtrude, like a faithful old dog, had never once complained or gone on strike, fact is she loves her name.

Just before leaving the stable, I patted her neck, and she gave me a nibble on the cheek.   On the way out I yelled goodnight to her, and she whinnied with an appreciative head nod. The old stableman spat a chew of tobacco into a pile of straw then looked from Gurtrude to me. After smiling at him I threw my saddlebag over my shoulder and started for the Hotel. The wind was loud, so I barely heard the old man yell after me, "Hey sonny," he said, "you two got any kids?"

The open street was a channel of bitter cold that stung my ears and bit cruelly at my nose and cheeks. The wind swirled and howled trying to frighten me, but its mean demonic wail was no match for the noisy piano and laughter coming from the bar at the Hotel. As I climbed the steps another smile slipped out.

The Teller House was a traveler's delight. The rooms were comfortable and for the most part private, but best of all; the place sported its own dining room and bar.

After signing the register, I checked the back pages for what might be a familiar name or two, but underneath it all I never really expected to see Tom's signature. He was too well known and by now word of his situation was out. Nowhere in Colorado would he be safe. Certainly, there would be friends and sympathizers, but always, and in large numbers, there would also be the heartless ones looking to cash in on another man's misfortune.

After paying the fee I asked for a signed receipt. My room was directly at the top of the stairs. While climbing I realized how tired I was. Once in the room I stripped to the waist and washed up, then shaved. There was a full house below and it was obvious a good time was being had by all.

The muffled chatter put a grin on my face as I recalled the night before Tom's wedding. A dozen of us had gotten him drunk then carried him over to the jail where we wrestled him down, stripped off every stitch of clothes except his boots, than cuffed him standing to a cell door. He surely was mad, but when we brought in the photographer, he was speechless. We figured a photo would be the ideal wedding gift for his new bride. It turned out she didn't see the humor. Fact is she wouldn't speak to any of us for three months. Of course, neither would Tom.

After slipping into a clean shirt, I pulled on my vest and pinned my badge beneath where it couldn't be seen unless I wanted it too. Then I strapped on the forty-four and left the room.

My stomach rumbled as I descended the Hotel stairs. Once at the foot I turned right and walked directly down into the saloon. The place was packed. Smoke was so thick you wondered how anyone could breathe. You couldn't hear yourself think for all the conversations and poker games, and the piano player was making obscene gestures as he banged out a tune for one of the saloon girls. The Teller House Bar was no place for a moral man…and I loved it.

CHAPTER TWO

Shaker Best was tending bar along with agent I didn't know. Shaker was a longtime friend of both Tom and me. He was a giant of a man with a chest like an oxen and monstrously large hands, and fortunate for many, a good-natured fellow. Most people looked up to him and I was one. Shaker wasn't his real name. I had heard talk of a time when he was deep into the Church way of life. Story goes, he belonged to some deep-south on-fire church that danced and waved in the isles during prayer meetings. One fellow said he heard it told Shaker had been known to roll on the floor when the spirit moved him.

While unable to imagine such a thing, I was never one to put down another for doing something he believes in, so I never asked him about it. Seeing him now though, behind the bar laughing and carrying on, I was certain about one thing; somewhere along the line he changed his denomination.

After I'd found a place to squeeze into at the bar, the gent I didn't know came over and asked my pleasure. I ordered a beer and told him to have Shaker step over first chance. He took my money, nodded, then poured me a mug.

The beer tasted good and slid down smoothly. My stomach was still growling, and I knew I'd have to feed it soon. Giving it a pat, I promised we'd eat as soon as I finished talking with Shaker.

With all the smoke in the air it seemed a silly thing to do, but I rolled a cigarette anyway. Taking my first draw I blew smoke across the bar watching it drift to a giant dingy mirror then up to a painting of a nude woman stretched out on a high headboard bed, smiling. I'd have liked a duplicate to hang in my office back in Denver but knew the mayor would strongly discourage the idea. Grinning, I shook my head.

When Shaker recognized me, he grinned and stuck out his hand. I took it but wished I hadn't. The giant squeezed until all the blood was gone, then squeezed a little more. The grin never left his face. He looked for the pain on mine but never saw it. Instead, I just gave him a grin right back.

Finally, he let go and spoke so loud even the Piano player could hear. "United States Marshall Archibald Steinberge, how in this crazy, human infested world have you been?"

Several of the men at the bar turned to look. I wasn't sure if it was because of the U.S. Marshall title, or my name. Each glanced up at my head to see what kind of hat I was wearing, then at my chest for a badge. But I gave them all a best turn back around look, then bestowed my attention back to Shaker.

"You enjoyed that didn't you?" I told him.

He tried giving me an innocent look. "What?"

"What," I said taking a sip of beer while working my numb fingers, "you know damn well I don't fancy being called, Archibald."

At that he laughed out loud, and everyone turned to look again.

"Arch," he went on, "a man should be proud of his name. It's his heritage."

Nodding with just a flicker of a smile I took another sip of beer.

"By the way," he asked loud enough for all to hear again, "how's Gertrude?"

Knowing the men around me were still listening and miners were worse than women when it came to gossip, I told him. "She's fine.

Trouble is she eats like a horse and has a belly like a rain barrel. Hell, I can't afford to feed her. Fact is, I'm thinking about getting rid of her. Maybe trade her to some drunken, half-blind miner. But hey, I didn't come here to talk about my sweetheart."

Shaker leaned on the bar with both arms. His face grew sober.

"You're looking for Tom, aren't you?"

"It's my job Shaker."

"To hell it is. They killed his family."

"I know," I said looking directly into his eyes, "but I lost his trail about two days ago. Besides, Tom isn't the only man I'm looking for."

Pulling out a sketch of Granger, I handed it to him. "You haven't seen this fellow, have you?"

Shaker stared at it a long while before answering. "Maybe I have. About four days ago, a man that looked similar stopped in for a quick whiskey. Didn't stay long, one drink and he was gone; had two other men with him."

"Did he say anything?"

Shaker nodded. "Yeah, said he'd rather be screwed by a donkey than spend another day in this iced over hell of a country." Shaker grinned a second then added, "Never heard it put quite like that before. That's the reason I remember him."

A dirty-faced miner chewing a huge plug yelled from down the bar for Shaker to bring him another beer, but Shaker told him to hold on.

"This man", Shaker went on, "had that mean look about him. Arch I don't think he'd be anyone to be messing with if you know what I mean?" Shaker pressed his lips tight together then asked, "Is he one of them that killed Tom's family?"

"Maybe? At least I think so. There were five total. Tom has tracked and killed four so far, but this one slipped away. I have no doubt Tom is trailing him."

Shaker looked me square in the eye and poked a big finger against my chest. "Then help him out. Hunt this son-of-a-biscuit eater down and kill him. Any man who could do what he did to other human beings, especially a woman and kids, don't deserve to live in our world, they belong in Hell."

He was right. But he failed to understand that I served the law and was a U.S. Marshall sworn to uphold it. I was not a self-appointed Bounty Hunter able to pick and choose if the person I hunted was brought in dead or alive.

Then Shaker grabbed my shoulder and pulled me to close enough to speak quietly in my ear. "Come on in the back room with me, Arch. I want to show you something."

My heart quickened. Was he taking me to Tom? Did he have him hidden away? After all, they were good friends. And if he did, what would I do? What would Tom do?

The impatient drinker down the bar yelled again, "Damn it Shaker, I'm empty down here." Releasing my shoulder, he pointed a finger. "Meet me at the end of the Bar."

On his way out he paused long enough to grab the impatient drinker with a giant hand pulling him half over the bar and yelling, "Don't you have any manners? I was talking with someone down there. If you're that damn thirsty swallow that chew puffing your cheek."

Shaker place his extra hand over his mouth and made a mean face. The miner's eyes grew big, and he swallowed. Shaker released him and yelled to the other tender, "Bill, pour this man a Beer on me."

It was difficult keeping up with Shaker for all the people. There must have been a hundred or more crowed like worms in a can. Shoulder to shoulder the men at the bar stood talking and drinking; some refined; dressed in expensive tailored suits; but most wore tattered miner's clothes with dirty faces and calloused hands. Every table was crowned with men playing cards and at least a dozen saloon girls in frilly, low-cut dresses working them with charm. The piano player pounded away endlessly.

With uneasiness I maneuvered my way through the standing bodies and around the tables. For the first time since entering the saloon I realized the smoke was burning my eyes.

Reaching down I tried the gun in my holster. A trickle of sweat streaked its way down the side of my face, and I realized too, for the first time, that it was actually hot in the saloon.

Caught up with Shaker, I followed him down a hallway and into a small room stacked with crates of whiskey. He must have seen the strain on my face and laughed.

"Hell man, you didn't think I had Tom hid out in here, did you?"

Clearing my throat, I looked up at him. "I guessed maybe I did, Shaker. Maybe I was hoping. Truth is I'd give about anything to talk with him right now."

"Well, I haven't got Tom, but I got something near as good. He was here. Said to tell you he heard this Granger fellow had a relative living in Tucson. Said he was going after him, said for you not to follow; said he loved ya."

Shaker paused making sure he remembered everything. "And oh ya," he added, "he told me to tell you not to sit your horse in the middle of an open field next time you're tracking an outlaw."

CHAPTER THREE

I sighed. So, Tom was safe! Relief washed over me like a cool waterfall on a hot dessert day. After thanking Shaker, I left the storeroom and returned to the bar. Ordering another beer, I lost myself in thought.

What was I to do now? Why had Tom left such a message? Did he really want me to follow, to catch up with him, maybe figuring he had a big enough lead to track down Granger, kill him, then turn himself into me for return to Denver? Or was he simply telling me he was okay, not to worry, that he trusted in our relationship enough to believe that I wouldn't follow. Taking a sip of beer I sighed, it was irksome trying to figure out the way other people think.

Nearly an hour passed before I got possession of a table. As soon as I was seated one of the saloon girls came over and took my order of steak and eggs. Her dress was cut so low, that when she leaned over her puppies nearly fell out; but she had a beautiful smile, so I didn't hold it against her. Following a handsome tip, she brought me another beer and promised to keep them coming.

Through the night the place never thinned out. For every man that left two came in to replace them. Just after midnight I watched four cowboys walk in together. None were dressed like miners or local businessmen; these cowboys wore yellow slickers over heavy coats, and each sported a narrow-brimmed hat, the kind preferred by cowboys from Montana or Wyoming territories where the wind blows frequent and wild; these for certain were not locals.

Once through the door they separated quickly moving off in different directions. Two took up positions at each end of the bar while a third positioned himself at the center. The fourth lingered near the door. I didn't like it and wanted to worn Shaker. Rising from my table I downed the last swallow of beer and started for the bar. That was when the one at the door pulled a shotgun from under his slicker and blasted the ceiling.   The sound echoed through the crowed room with roaring confusion. Instantly the piano music, the laughter and every bit of conversation stopped. The place fell quiet as a funeral parlor. Heads turned as shocked eyes searched for the source of the blast.

The man who had fired the shotgun yelled loud, clearing up any wonder, "Easy boys" In the same instant his two partners at each end of the bar scrambled on top of it for perfect observation over the crowd. They too pulled shotguns from beneath their slickers. The fellow in the middle remained where he was.

The leader at the door began moving to the center of the room waving the barrel of his gun; the crowd of once happy drinkers hastily opened a path. "As you all can see," he said, "this is a holdup. Keep your mouths shut and hands away from them guns. You men at the tables put your hands on top of it and lay em flat. As for all you boys at the bar, get down on the floor and stretch your arms out in front of you." There was hesitation and slight mumbles of protest. "Now, damn it!" he yelled, "the rest of you up against the wall with your hands on it reaching for the ceiling. And do it quick."

The sound of men scrambling to their bellies and boot heels clicking against the wood floor exploded to life as we each moved into the positions ordered. With the beer mug still in my hand I moved to the wall and raised my arms like the others.

"Now noses to the wall and hands flat." He demanded. We each did as told. "My man will come around with a bag. When he gets to you, one at a time, lower your hands and be so kind as to empty your pockets for him."

The bar was silent and although our backs were to him, we could hear the movement of the fellow with the bag. By the time the third or fourth victim had emptied his pockets the sound of jingling coins marked his every step.

A hundred men were in the bar, at least half I'd guess were no stranger to a gun, and we were all being held at bay by only four of the same. We could take these men I knew, but not without risk and I had no right to ask anyone to help. Taking risks was my job, not theirs. I couldn't help thinking though, that if Tom were here with me, we'd put a fast end to it all.

Outside, above the silence of the room the wind moaned and swirled in the cold street rattling the door. And it was snowing, making this the perfect robbery; the hard falling snow would make a perfect cover as it buried their tracks. These men were no greenhorns. They knew when to hit and had probably waited for the heavy fall before making their move. My guess would be that they knew the area too. Once they walked out that door there would be little chance of recovering the losses.

There were twenty or so of us standing against the wall with raised arms. Shaker and his helper had been ordered out from behind the bar and made to lay down with the others. I couldn't expect any help from them.

Suddenly the sound of a chair scraping the floor was heard, followed by the boot heels of a running man. From the corner of my eye, I caught a glimpse of someone scrambling toward the door leading out into the street. He had been close to it but I knew he'd never make it. The shotgun roared and its sound deafened us all. The buckshot was close patterned and its impact tore hard into the running man's back. His body hurtled forward crashing through the big glass window just to the right of the door. Fragments flew everywhere and the sound of breaking glass was quickly drowned by the sudden inward gush of wild wind and snow flurries. The incoming wind was strong and now its roar was loud; but the man in charge yelled above its howl.

"Anybody else want to be a stupid hero?"

I didn't think hero was the case at all. The runner had been a young fellow; too scared to sweat it out. His body lay half out in the street with only his legs showing at the window. I felt anger and my jaws tightened; that killing had been senseless.

The man with the bag was finished with the group on the floor and was now working the wall. Using the sound of the jingling coins, I gauged his distance, and through peripheral vision, watched him work closer to my position. He was working his way down the row to my left. The beer mug was in my right hand, and I wanted it free to get to my gun. I had to change hands and my arms were wide apart. In my brain a plan was forming. Sometimes a plan takes thinking for long hours, then other times, like now, it comes from the gut, more like a reaction.

As far as I was concerned, these men weren't just stealing now; they were murderers. The young boy running for the door could have been shot in the legs or given a warning. Instead, he had been gunned down in cold blood. So now, no matter what, these four men would go to jail or meet the devil right here in the Teller House.

The wind continued to howl through the shattered window and a thin layer of snow was piling up on the end of the bar. The fellow with the bag was three men down. Slowly I inched my hands together until finally, very easily, I switched the mug. When he was one man from me, I took a deep breath and waited. The coins jingled in the sack and as I stared at the wall, I wondered if the others were watching us; there was no way of knowing short of turning around, but I guessed not; a hundred men, most with guns, were a lot of people to watch.

The two at the end of the bar were still there, on top in clear view. The gunman in the middle of the floor was just behind me somewhere; I had only his voice as a clue. He was maybe eight or ten feet away and would be my first target.

When the bag-man's hand touched my shoulder the heavy glass mug came down hard as I whirled. It caught him across the face, and he screamed as my arm went around his neck and I pulled him to me. Simultaneously my gun came out of its holster and the first bullet took the mouthy one in the chest. Beyond him at the far end of the bar, I took down my second target. He toppled backwards crashing into a layer of bottles then falling lifeless somewhere behind the bar.

One was left! He was the real danger. Even as the colt came around in my hand the shotgun blast erupted; its buckshot scattering into an ever-widening pattern as it rushed toward me. For the most part, it ripped into the chest of the man I held in front of me, but some of the pellets tore into my left arm and I felt the stinging pain the same instant I fired. I missed but from somewhere in the pile of men on the floor, a shot rang out, one that didn't miss, and I knew someone had come to my aid. The last of the four men fell hard to the floor, sprawled out on his back.

As if stunned, everyone remained where they were for nearly a full minute. For a few seconds the smell of gun smoke lingered, but the wind quickly carried it off. Then slowly, men began moving. They rose from the floor and arms lowered; chairs scraped against the floor as they left their tables. Chatter was slow at first but soon the place buzzed with noisy conversation again.

Some men came to shake my hand and give their thanks while others went about gathering material with which to board up the shattered window. Shaker ordered others to take the bodies of the dead men to the undertaker. He sent another for the Doc. A large group of the remaining men pulled a table over to where I stood and set me in a chair. Blood was dripping from my fingertips, but I'd been hurt worse. In the blink of an eye a dozen beers sat on the table in front of me. What could I do, holding one up, I grinned in appreciation and toasted their hospitality; again, and again and again.

The wound had turned out minor, so the Doc bandaged it, drank a beer with me, then was gone. Within a short time, my steak and potatoes arrived, and I ate them in a hurry. It wasn't until past three I managed to slip away.

Back in the room I pulled off my boots and stretched out on the bed. While lying there, my thoughts, like the room, swirled and wouldn't leave me alone.

In Denver there awaited my office, my job, and my responsibilities. In Tucson, I'd find Tom, who I really didn't want to find, and maybe Granger, whom I did. And ironically, if it was Tom I found, a good man, a fine lawman… he'd probably hang. And if it was Granger, a worthless human being, a killer…he would probably go free.

Turning onto my side I blew out the lantern; the room went dark and suddenly I felt so alone. Rolling back, I listened to the rope network creak beneath. Staring into the black ceiling I sighed. "Well Arch," I whispered to myself, "it's damned if you do and damned if you don't." I laid there a long time thinking and spinning as if tied to a windmill. Then goodness came, sleep took me away.

CHAPTER FOUR

I departed Central City beneath a beautiful morning sky. Having allowed myself the luxury of sleeping late, the eight o'clock morning sun now shined bright. The white snow shimmered with an almost blinding luster and Gertrude was spunky, having appreciated the good night's rest. The streets were busy with morning activity. Merchants were out shoveling snow and miners passed frequently on the boardwalks and in the snowy streets on their way to and from work. Orr wagons clamored up the hilly roadways often slipping and sliding to the yell of their drivers. Smoke rose from chimneys only to be blown away by a soft morning breeze; and behind me I could hear the clamoring of a school bell.

Stopping in at the telegraph office, I sent a gram to Denver, telling them of my decision; that I was remaining in pursuit of Tom Wade. I never mentioned Granger or his relatives in Tucson. I did not wish for the Sheriff's Office there to know anything, not yet anyway, and I was afraid one of my deputies might take it upon himself to send them a message.

Tom would probably be traveling by horseback, not chancing a finger-pointing on a train or stage. It had crossed my mind to take the train myself and beat him into Tucson by a few days, but I nixed the idea. If I picked up his trail, there was a fair chance I could catch him before he got there. Besides, I thought, if he were to alter his plans and decide not to go in that direction, I could end up waiting in the city of Tucson until my hair thinned.

So, reining south, I followed along the mountains until the turnoff for Leadville. Tom would need supplies and maybe he would chance a stop there. It was worth a try. I needed a lead and had nothing to lose. My guess was that he would follow the divide down to Pagosa Springs then over to Durango, moving down into New Mexico toward Gallup, then turn west into Arizona and on down to Tucson. A man always leaves a trail, even Tom Wade. Besides, I knew how he tracked and covered his trail. We were a lot alike.

It was easy traveling for most of the trip into Leadville. Three times I had come across lone riders heading into the Denver area. Only one had mentioned seeing a rider fitting Tom's description. He had said the man seemed uneasy but had offered him coffee and an evening meal. And he said too, that this same man had inquired about the identity of a fellow he was following. So I knew I was on the right path. Based on the information the man had told me, Tom was about a day and a half ahead of me. We were at least a week out of Tucson, so I felt confident I could catch him.

Leadville turned up nothing. No sign of Tom being there. The local merchant had sold no supplies out of the ordinary, so after a good meal, I headed south along the Arkansas river toward Salida. Following along the river, I could travel through the night and markedly close the gap between us.

At dark I stopped and built a small fire. After putting over a pot of coffee, I rolled a cigarette then sat back to enjoy it. The night around me was black with only a handful of stars in the sky. It was quiet and bitterly cold. To my back I could hear the swift current of the Arkansas.

The coffee was hot, so I poured a cup and sipped it, liking the way it helped chase away the cold. With a shiver, I pulled up the collar of my coat then wrapped my hands around the warm coffee cup. Around me the wind howled, a lonely cry. I took another sip then tossed my cigarette to the side.

Life was strange and too often it dealt us a bad hand. It's said the rain falls on the good and bad alike; I believed that to be true. Tom Wade and Granger were good examples.

Although only a split second of sound, it was sufficient time for my brain to realize what it was. Following the loud report, the hot chunk of lead flew out of the darkness slicing open the right side of my skull. Bone crunched, but only for a second did I feel pain. Though sitting, I felt myself falling backwards toward the cold, waiting snow. And as I fell, I could feel myself slipping deeper and deeper into a world even blacker than the desolate darkness around me. And just before unconsciousness carried me away, I cursed myself for having built a fire.

How long I lay unconscious was impossible to guess. When I came around, I realized I was shaking…freezing. My vision was blurred, and my head felt like it was on fire. There was no strength in my body, so I had no choice but lie in the wet snow and shiver. Disoriented, I tried to rationalize, to unscramble the bundle of twisted thoughts knotted together in my brain. Someone had tried to kill me…who? And why; and where were they now?

The air was cold; I was cold; freezing. Why wasn't I dead? Wasn't it dark? Now it was light. Through squinted eyes I could make out a blue sky. How long had I been out?

Suddenly I felt a boot heel on my shoulder and the force of it caused me more pain. The sun was bright, and I squinted to see who it was. Slowly my sight came into focus… it was Granger.

Behind him stood two other men I didn't know. He was smiling arrogantly, and I hated the sight of him. His words to me were filled with contempt and sarcasm.

"Marshal Steinberge! A little out of our territory, aren't we?"

I didn't reply.

He pulled his boot from my shoulder and tapped it cruelly against the open wound on my head. I wanted to scream from the pain, but I held it in.

"Poor fellow," He continued. "Looks like you're in bad shape. "Looks of your head, I'd say somebody tried to kill you. I can't imagine anyone trying to do in a Federal Marshall, though." At that he glanced over his shoulder at the two men with him. "Can you boys?" They laughed and played it up. I spoke for the first time.

"Granger," I said, mustering the strength to talk. "No doubt your mother was an ugly female jackass and at delivery, shit you out."

This time he didn't find things so humorous. His boot toe slammed into my ribs and the pain was almost unbearable. Groaning, I grit my teeth.

"You think you're so great, don't you, Mr. U.S. Marshall? Well let me tell you something; you're the shit. In fact, you know what you are…"

I cut him off. "Yeah, I know what I am, a man who doesn't have to shoot people in the head to be able to kick in their ribs."

His face grew red, "You son of a bitch, Steinberge." Finger pointed, he added, "I was going to kill you, but now I don't think so. Instead, I'll let you live; that is, live long enough to watch me hunt down and kill that worthless deputy of yours. The one who thinks he's hot on my trail. I'm going to hang him by his feet with hands tied behind his back; then slowly slit his throat. And after he's all bled out, I'll drown you in his blood."

"You're a sick man, Granger." I said coldly.

He laughed. "And you're a soon to be dead man, Steinberge. Get him up!"

They pulled me to my feet and my head pounded. Positioning himself in front of me, Granger pulled his knife and held the cutting edge to the side of my throat.

"We need to slow you up a bit." He spoke.

I wanted to kick him, but I couldn't find the strength. Then he pulled the knife slowly across my neck and I felt the sting of the cut as flesh opened. Blood rolled down my shoulder. Grabbing a hand full of hair, he pinned my head back and got in my face for what was going to be a dramatic word, but it never came. I spit on him instead. He didn't see the humor.

As the others held me, his fists flew in a wild rampage; first to my face, a left then a right; then to my body and back to my face. Pain raged over every inch of me and there was no catching my breath. He had knocked the wind out of me, and I thought I'd never breathe again. Blood filled my mouth followed by numbness. Finally, there came the last blow…a hard fist straight into the gunshot wound on the side of my head. It added a new dimension of agony, but it was of little consequence. The two men let go and I fell in a heap.

The snow felt good, and its coldness kept me from passing out. In a state of fogginess, the world had become a distant, faraway place, a land of strange and blurry shapes. Through eyes I could feel swelling shut, I could make out Granger's form as he leaned over me and flipped open my coat. As he ripped the badge from my shirt he laughed, his voice edged with challenge.

"You want this back Mr. Big Time Lawman, come and get it."

My ears picked up muffled laughter then I was alone. Lying helpless in the cold snow, I tried to reason. Things did not look good for me. Death was not far away. As I lay there motionless, I could feel warm blood seep from my head wound. I was also bleeding from my neck and my ribs hurt with each breath I took. My eyes would be swelled shut in a short time. I wanted to move, I needed to move. But it seemed impossible; there was no strength and no coordination. My body was shivering vigorously, but I noted that as a good sign; so long as I shivered, there was warmth inside my body; if it stopped, I would be dead in minutes.

What needed to be done was clear. Get to where it was warm, care for my wounds, sleep, eat, drink and regain my strength. To remain here, motionless in the cold wet snow was sure death. Lying on my back, I could feel the warm sun on my face, but it was not enough to help. To my left lay the remains of last night's fire, maybe I could get to it for a rekindle. It was my only chance.

Slowly I turned my head and looked, judging the distance. It was there, a dark blurry mass, five maybe six feet away. Somewhere far off in the distance a lone bird called out as it sailed through a sky rich with blue.

First, I wiggled my fingers then worked my feet. Each breath was an effort, and I knew I had broken ribs. My legs flexed all right and arms worked with concentration. Inside my head were entangled chains of thought while on the outside I felt like a broken wagon wheel—all the pieces there but shattered and useless.

Painstakingly I began to inch my way toward the cold remains of the fire. As I moved, new waves of cold rippled through me and what little bit of body heat I had left was going quickly. It would be a race; the rekindling of the fire before the body heat was gone.

My slow crawling body left deep furrows in the snow as I forged closer to my one chance. My teeth chattered. Inside my body there was pain and numbness mixed. No leaps and bounds in my movements, only small inches of progress. Time moved in slow agonizing segments, it was barely noticeable progress, then rest. I teetered back and forth between life and death, unsure of whose side I wanted to be on. Through closed swollen eyes I could tell the sun was rising higher in the sky above. It would mean a little more warmth, but I didn't need a little more, I needed a lot more.

With a trembling left hand, I reached out and touched the black remains of the old fire…I was there! In my coat were matches. Reaching down slowly I groped for the pocket and found it. In went my hand, slowly, shaking. I touched them the same time the dark shadow fell across me. Then I heard the crunching of snow as someone took three steps before stopping to stare. There was no way of seeing who it was, they were standing beyond my head, and I couldn't turn. Besides, my eyes were nearly sealed shut now. In my head I had a good idea who it was. He had probably been standing off in the distance watching my struggles, laughing, and now was back to finish what he had started.

My pistol was in its holster, but it may as well have been a mile away. I wanted to see, to look in his disgusting face. I wanted to put a bullet in him. Then filtering through the endless waves of pain I realized I had heard no other sounds, no laughing or mocking. Maybe it wasn't Granger! God, I thought, could it be Tom come to rescue me?

Then I laughed. Tom was far away riding for Arizona with no idea I was laying here in the winter snow dying; so, what did it matter, what did anything matter. Besides, it was too late; cold was fading and the warmth of death was racing its way up my body...bringing with it that very long, peaceful rest.

CHAPTER FIVE

Tom Wade was a sight for sore eyes…literally.

My lids were swollen, but I managed a squinty left eye peak just enough to make out his blurry form as he knelled. It was a short painful gesture, but I extended my hand. He took it, and made a pitiful smile, at least I guessed it was a smile. I attempted smiling back, as best I could. Bless the man, he lightheartedly tried to make the best of a not so good situation; "I got to tell you Arch", he told me, "You haven't looked this bad since the morning after my wedding."

I wanted to say something funny in return, but it was all I could do just to breath. Tom patted my shoulder gently. "You take it easy partner, just savior the pain you probably earned, leave everything else to me."

I remember him leaving and returning with a couple of blankets. After wrapping me up he was gone again. I slept restlessly from that point on, waking only for brief spurts of time, confused and disoriented only to return once again to that dark, empty world of nothingness. It was in and out, awake then asleep; those little slices of death stealing away precious moments of life.

I wanted to stay awake, to climb in the saddle and ride after Granger. God knew I wanted him. And I wanted to talk with Tom, but I had no control, no strength. Time passed me by and I had no idea in what quantity, perhaps minutes or hours, or even days for that matter.

My mind, in between dreams, remained a cluttered mass of thought and questions. I could tell my body burned with fever and sweat relentlessly soaked my covers.

I lay in a dark room and could feel the warmth of a nearby fire. Several times I remembered being fed broth and small sips of water. In my half awake, half a sleep states, I tossed and turned moaning and crying, reliving much of my past in strange worlds filled with twisted faces and impossible feats. I cried out and wept with sorrow and laughed too. Like a prisoner I was locked within my own body just out of reach of consciousness.

Death had come and stood over me, waiting; but I fought with it, wrestled with it; battled it with all the strength I could muster. Then finally, staring it straight in the face, I ordered it back into hell. It was then that I awoke.

Tom was sitting at my side. Looking at me he grinned. "Well, it's about time you opened your eyes. I see little has changed; you still like to sleep late."

Though it hurt I smiled, telling him from my heart. "I owe you."

Tom shook his head, "No way. Remember that time up in the Bitter Route Range, when we were tracking the foster gang?" I nodded and he went on. "They would have gutted me if you hadn't come charging in like some kind of one-man army, shooting and shouting. Consider us even. Now, how do you feel?"

Wetting my swollen lips with my tongue, I told him, "Like you shot me out of a cannon straight into a stone wall."

"Think you can eat something?" Tom asked.

All that fever and sweating had created a hunger in me. "You bet I can. "

"Good." Squeezing my shoulder Tom rose and walked away.

Glad to be awake, I took the time to look around. I was lying on a board bunk in a small, one room cabin: probably a line shack. A small fireplace to my right burned brightly, casting shadows over the walls and ceiling. Tom was leaning over a pot of stew there and dishing me out a small bowl. The place had one window and it had been boarded up. The door was rickety and filled with gaps, and it was obvious it had been repaired more than once over the years. A strong wind outside rattled it and whistled in through the cracks, but I didn't care; Tom Wade would keep it warm.

My wounds had been cleaned and bandaged, and wide strips of cloth had been tied securely around my ribs, making it easier for me to breathe.

Tom returned with the stew, so I pulled myself to a sitting position with a grimace and took the bowl from his hands. It hurt when I moved but at least I was still able. In between bites, Tom and I talked.

It was only by chance he'd found me. Granger had doubled back in an attempt to lose Tom, but there was no way. While hot on Grangers' trail, Tom happened upon me by accident; he built a travois and brought me here.

With the stew half eaten, I handed the bowl back to Tom and lay down again. Turning my head, I looked at him and said in a tired tone, "I guess you're some kind of a miracle worker, Thomas Wade."

He laughed softly, "No, not really, just a lot of prayer and strong constitution on your part."

Reaching out, I grasped his forearm. "Tom." I said soberly. "I want Granger as bad as you do."

"Maybe," he said, looking directly into my eyes. "But there's a lot of hate inside of me, Arch. I don't just want to kill him; I want to do it slowly and with my bare hands." Not batting an eye, his jaws tightened. "Promise me Arch, when the time comes you won't interfere."

What could I say? That the beating I took was more important than the slaughter of his family, or that his saving my life counted for nothing? Sure, I was the law and Tom was on the wrong side of it. But now, at least for the time being, the human element took precedence. Besides, I was thinking that there just might be a way around all of this.

Letting go of Tom's arm, I said, "Say no more. You're under arrest." His jaws went slack then tight again.

In a voice mixed with anger and disbelief, he replied. "You're kidding…aren't you?"

"Look." I began. "It's my job to arrest you, right?" He nodded, not sure of my point, and I went on. "As the arresting officer, I order you to help me track down and apprehend the criminal known as Granger, wanted for the attempted murder of a Federal Marshal. And as my prisoner, I give you full right to carry your six-gun. Once the criminal has been put in chains or disposed of properly, you will surrender both your gun and you to me. Is that agreeable?"

He stared at me, and began to grin, "Agreed." He said, "But one thing. What exactly do you mean by, disposing of Granger properly?"

For a long time, we stared. Just what exactly did I mean, I wondered? While Tom waited for the answer, I did some soul searching. Really, was there an answer? It would have been easy to say kill him when you find him, he certainly deserved it. But what if every man decided to bypass the law and do whatever he considered right? It was funny, I thought, the law, if allowed to mix with human emotion, often became an entangled web of impossible rules, and yet without it, appeared cold and heartless. Sighing, I finally told him. "Let's cross that open field when we get to it, okay?

Tom stuck out his hand and I took it. It sent a good feeling through me.

"Okay," he said warmly, "One open field at a time. And right now, the only one we must cross is getting you back on your feet. Get some rest!"

He was right. Now, I felt very tired and wanted nothing more than to sleep, to sleep a long time; then wake up all better and ready to ride… after Granger.

Closing my eyes, I sighed. A feeling of easiness washed over me and for the first time in days I felt myself relax.

CHAPTER SIX

When I awoke, the fire was out, and rays of sunlight were filtering in through the cracks of the cabin door. It was quiet and I realized Tom was gone. The place was cold, and a second long twitch shot through me. Slowly, I sat up swinging my feet over the side of the bunk. My head began to pound, so I sat still for a few minutes. Then, pulling the blanket tight around me, I stood to my feet.

Pain stabbed into my ribs, but I worked my way to where my coat hung and pulled a couple of matches from the pocket. Slowly, with easy steps, I worked my way to the cold remains of the fire and rekindled it. The flames grew fast and felt good. Sitting down on the stone hearth for support, I warmed my hands. There was no way of knowing how long Tom had been gone; the fire had been out at least two hours. And just how long I'd been asleep, there was no guessing either, but what I did know for sure, was that I was hungry again.

Rising to my feet, I eased my way over to a corner of the cabin where Tom had our gear stacked. Rummaging through it, I found some hardtack and jerked beef. The hardtack was worth a try, but the jerked beef would require too much chewing, my sore face was not up to that. So after digging out some leftover stew from the pot, I ate it along with a bit of hardtack.

This time, I ate heartily. When finished, I set the empty bowl on the table and made my way to the door. Holding my ribs with one hand, I opened it with the other. Outside the day was bright and there was freshness in the air. The cabin sat on a hillside overlooking the distant mountains. There was peace here, and I thought how sad it was the whole world couldn't be like this. To the right of the cabin, I heard a horse whinny and smiled. I'd recognize that outcry anywhere.

Painstakingly slipping on my boots and coat, I went outside and walked around to where Gertrude waited. It felt good to be out in the fresh air again. She recognized me right away and shook her head with excitement. When close enough, she sniffed first, then snorted and nudged me several times. Patting her neck, I looked around for Tom's horse, but it was gone. He was probably out hunting fresh meat, and that sounded good to me. My appetite was coming back so there was no mistaking it, I was on the mend.

Returning to the cabin, I put another log on the fire then lay back down. While staring into the flames, I thought about Tom. It was good seeing him again; I really missed his companionship. He had been the best deputy I'd ever worked with, not to mention being my closest friend. There was nothing I wanted more than to somehow clear his name; but that would not be easy. My only chance was to get to Granger and keep him alive long enough for a confession in front of a witness...although Tom had different ideas; if he got to him first, his hatred and thirst for revenge would ruin it all and he would condemn himself to the gallows. Granger, on the other hand, was no one to underestimate. He was a cold-blooded killer, a killer who was looking forward to meeting up with Tom too, only he wanted it to be on his own terms.

How could I possibly prevent such an inevitable meeting; this would be a clash of pure hatred? When it happened, all of hell itself would take a front seat to watch. Closing my eyes, I let out a long sigh. Tom Wade. I said his name several times under my breath while thinking out possible solutions to the problem. And sometime during all that thinking, the sweet touch of sleep came once again putting my troubled mind at rest.

A soft noise startled me awake. My eyes were blurry, so I blinked them into focus. Tom was at the fire tending a frying pan. The same instant I saw him, my nose smelled the frying rabbit; it made my stomach growl, and I realized how famished I was.

Lying still, I took a few minutes to clear away the cobwebs in my brain. All the sleeping I'd been doing, though good, was keeping my mind in a state of mild confusion.

There remained some swelling in my face, but much to my satisfaction it was quickly diminishing. As for the gunshot wound, it was healing nicely and even my ribs were easing in pain. I had a lot to be thankful for and certainly owed my life to Tom.

When he turned from the fire and saw me awake, he gestured with the steaming frying pan held in his hands, "Fried rabbit and hardtack smothered in gravy, followed with a good cup of hot coffee. What do you say?"

What could I say! Next to fried chicken, rabbit was my favorite. Giving him a nod of approval, I pulled myself to a sitting position. Tom placed the hot pan on the table and glanced my way.

"Think you can see your way clear to sit at the table?"

My answer was quick. "For fried rabbit I'll tie myself to the chair."

Flashing a grin, Tom turned and threw a log on the fire while I lowered my legs over the side of the bed.

He was some kind of man, I thought. It wasn't that long ago we had been at his home where his wife Caroline had cooked us a big Sunday dinner of fried rabbit. There had been more food than we could have dreamed of eating. Caroline had been an excellent cook. She had baked us an apple pie and I had embarrassed myself by eating almost the entire thing before leaving that night.

Before all of this happened, Tom had been a blessed man. As I watched him working about the cabin, fetching this and that, setting the table, pouring the coffee and all else, I wondered if he was remembering the same thing I was. Then he looked up and grinned.

"Come and get it and bring your manners with you." With no great speed, I made my way to the table and grimaced myself onto a chair. The mixed aroma of the rabbit and coffee caused hunger pains way down deep in the pit of my stomach. Tom didn't have to say 'dig in' twice.

There was no stopping me. I probably looked a sight, but my body was hungry, needing the nourishment of the food. Tom watched me from across the table, grinning. "You know," he said amusingly, "It's a good thing you're able to feed yourself. If I had to spoon you, I'd probably end up losing a finger."

"My, aren't we the funny one," I said. "Here I sit, having been beaten to within an inch of my life, shot in the head with a rifle, maybe slowly bleeding this very minute on the inside, and you crack jokes. For all you know funny Mr. Wade, I might be dying."

"Could be," he said with a short burst of laughter. "But if you do, I am not burying you, the ground's too hard."

I lifted my coffee cup, "To friendship."

Outside snow was falling hard again and a harsh wind continuously blew in through the cracks of the cabin door. The fire was warm though, and the interior of the small line shack remained comfortable. As soft shadows danced on the walls around us, we talked.

Tom took a sip of coffee then looked across the table.

"You know, Arch. It strikes me as strange that Granger left you alive. It just isn't his way."

Clearing my throat, I looked Tom straight in the eyes. There was no sense in pussyfooting around. He was a grown man and had had his share of hard riding. Besides, he had a right to know what awaited him.

"Granger wants you as bad as you want him, Tom. Says he's going to wait till the time's right, then cut your throat and drown me in your blood," I watched his reaction closely, but his expression never changed. "Actually, "I went on, "I've been giving it a lot of thought. I mean, why, would anyone in their right mind attempt to kill a U.S. Marshall by first shooting him, then beating him to within an inch of his life; and do it all in the open?"

"It's obvious," Tom said. "He wants both of us…together. Otherwise, he would have left you dead back there in the snow."

"Exactly," I cut in. "So, let's give it some thought. The man's no fool. We're close and he knows it; and he knows just what I'm thinking; that if I can get to him before you and get a confession, you're off the hook; and at the same time, your only intention is to kill him in cold blood, at any cost."

Tom took another sip of coffee, "Yeah. It kind of pits us one against the other, doesn't it?"

I nodded, "Looks that way."

"In other words," Tom went on, "So long as you keep him alive, I have a chance. But if you kill him, or I kill him; it kills me, in a manner of speaking."

"Exactly." Taking a bite of rabbit, I chewed then swallowed. "He's a smart one Tom, no doubt. Now I have to ask you, have you given any thought at all for a chance at a reprieve? I mean; is killing him worth the only chance you have?"

His face grew hard and in his eyes, I saw a look I'd never seen before. There was hate in his voice. "The man killed my family Arch: my daughter, my son and my wife. He raped Caroline then burned them all up in the house; didn't even have the compassion to leave me their bodies for a decent burial."

Tom's eyes filled with wetness and his lip quivered as he spoke. In his voice there was pain. "Arch, when I found them, they…" He looked away a few seconds then returned his eyes to mine. A single tear streaked down his cheek, and I pretended not to see it. "When I found them, they were little more than charred pieces of meat. My God, I could barely recognize them."

Unable to say any more, he stood up and left the table-walking over to face the fire. As he stood there staring into the flames, I felt helpless. I knew there were tears in his eyes and unbearable pain in his heart. I knew too, that killing had deepened deep down into his soul. I wondered why God allowed scum like Granger to live and breathe; and good men like Tom Wade to have to face such grief and anguish.

Leaving the table, I walked to his side and put a hand on his shoulder. What was there to say? How could I help him? Then Tom turned and looked into my eyes - and for the first time in our lives, I saw him break down and cry out loud. He threw his arms around me, and I held him. For a long time, he wept. And all the while his tears fell, my heart grew heavy too, and like him, the only truly satisfying answer seemed to be in hunting Granger down; and upon finding him, killing him in pure, unadulterated cold blood...slowly!

It was six more days before I was able to ride. The swelling in my face was practically gone and I had removed the bandaging from my head; nothing left there now but an inch long scar hidden beneath my hair; my hat still fit so I was happy. As for the ribs, the pain had localized to a small spot on the right side.

Feeling like a new man, I smiled as we swung up into our saddles. When I was seated, Gertrude whinnied, and I patted her neck. The sun was warm, and the sky was rich with color. It was a beautiful morning, and I was glad to be part of it. I was happy too, that Tom Wade and I were riding together again. The air was fresh, and I took a deep breath. It filled me with an energetic sense of confidence. I knew we'd find Granger soon, and when we did, things would somehow work out for the best. It just had to!

Reining south we rode until we picked up the Arkansas River again. We'd follow it down to Saliva where maybe, if lucky, we'd turn up a lead. There was no way of knowing for sure which way Granger went; he may have turned north and headed back to Denver for all we knew, although we doubted it. He was never popular there to begin with and now, because of what he had done, it was not safe for him.

If it was true about his having a relative in Tucson, then probably that was where he was headed. At least we hoped so, because that was our destination unless we picked up a trail.

Granger had a good week's ride on us now, although it really didn't matter. He wanted Tom Wade, wanted him on his own terms and in his own sweet time, and he wanted the satisfaction of finishing me off too. Looking up into the blue sky I watched the drifting clouds a minute, then sighed. Sure as the Devil himself was straw-boss in Hell; a fight was coming. And just as sure as Gertrude was the love of my life, when that fight found us, not only would I be ready; I was more than willing.

CHAPTER SEVEN

As the horses strolled, Tom and I talked. He had been raised the son of a career Army Officer; along with two sisters and a younger brother. His mother was a soft-spoken Christian woman who had seen to it they attended church regularly while growing up. At age seventeen Tom left home to try his hand at college; in part to his father's prodding; but after two years realized the academic life was not for him and struck out on his own.

He took a job scouting for the Army and at the outbreak of the War Between the States enlisted as an infantryman. Although he didn't say what had happened; at the Battle of Bull Run he received a battlefield commission straight to Captain. Later serving under Sherman he climbed to the rank of Major and stayed there until the war ended. Once again a civilian, he worked a while for the railroad as a surveyor then moved to St. Louis and ran a mercantile for a couple of years. From there he relocated to Denver taking the job of Deputy and met Caroline. After nearly nine years of happily married life and two beautiful children, along came Granger.

As for my story there had been no college, not even a chance at it. I came from a poor upstate New York Jewish family and at the age of fourteen quit school to help run our dairy farm. With a love for learning though, I picked up every book I could get my hands on. My dream had always been to go to Law School, but too often fate takes the reins and even though your heart wants to ride north, you end up going south.

It turned out dairying grew to repetitious. At sixteen, practically disowned by my father, I left the farm and rode west. With a mix of good sense and a bit of luck, I did manage to paddle my own canoe; taking whatever job I could get; I cow-punched a couple of years, candy-danced a season, scouted for a couple of wagon trains, and worked the silver minds of Colorado. And somewhere in the mix of it all I learned to use a gun better than most; and although never once pulled it on a man who didn't deserve it; more than once I'd hired it out for a place to lay my head. Can't really say I can put a finger on it, but somewhere in those long hard years of growing, the badge I would one day take back from Granger, got pinned to my shirt.

We covered nearly fifteen miles before dusk slipped in around us. In the western sky the sun formed a perfect ball and painted the horizon the color of blood; it made me think of Granger.

Riding upon the remains of an old adobe shack, we made camp for the night. The building had been a narrow, two room affair; on one side the roof had long ago caved in and was now buried beneath the winter snow, the remaining section, however, was still intact with a good roof and three sides. It also contained a workable fireplace. The dwelling would do nicely for the night.

Across the open end we stretched my lean-to canvas and locked out a lot of the cold. While Tom built a fire, I stripped the horses of gear and stacked it inside. The animals themselves I tied around the back out of sight and out of the wind.

Supper consisted of hard-tack and jerky. When finished, we poured a cup of coffee and sat back. The fire crackled and threw out a cozy-warmth. I rolled a smoke and stretched out. In the heavens above us the sky glittered with stars, and except for the soft crackling of the fire there was total quiet; and at least for now, a satisfying contentment. Leaned against our saddles Tom and I sipped our coffee in silence, each lost in his own thoughts.

I wondered the outcome of the day when we finally did meet up with Granger and his cohorts. He was a hard man, cruel and certainly no one to underestimate. His blood ran cold, and I knew that if our guns were held to the other's head, he would not hesitate to pull the trigger. The question was…would I?

Tom sat staring into the flames of the fire–something he would not normally do while tracking someone, for he knew only too well how the beauty of it steals away night vision; but this fire was not one to draw anyone's attention, no one could see it but he and I; we were, for the time being, concealed and safe.

I knew where Tom's thoughts were, and I understood. Besides, my eyes were on the tarp that opened to the dark world on the other side. There was no need for Tom to worry; let him sit and lose himself within his memories. His face told me they were good ones, at least for the moment, for he was sitting with his coffee growing cold in its cup and a soft smile across his face; a smile warm as the flames into which he stared.

It was around six when we swung into the saddles. The sky was still dark but over the eastern mountains a gray light was beginning to show. We could see our breath and beneath the horses the hard snow crunched against their weight. The air was cold and bit the skin we couldn't cover. Wind whistled out of the north, but it was little more than a whisper, and for that we were thankful.

For the first hour we rode in silence acclimating ourselves to the new day. Tom, who ordinarily was clean cut and shaven was taking on a new look. He had cultivated a well-groomed beard and was letting his hair grow long. And somewhere along the way, before his finding me in my sorrowful state, he acquired a pair of dark rimmed reading glasses; purchased to ware when around other people; like those looking for him. Of this I was glad, because when he put them on it made me laugh. I told him as soon as his hair grew down to his shoulders, I'd have to start calling him Ben Franklin. As a disguise though, the new change would serve him well.

CHAPTER EIGHT

The town of Salida laid ahead three- or four-hours ride. It was another small town filled with men and women who lived for gossip. If Granger had come through, we'd know soon enough.

The further south we rode the more the Terrain began to change. The steep, tree covered slopes were now behind us and here there were gentle, rolling hills, scantily spotted with pine dark against the white backdrop. We were in cattle country here and as we rode; we watched them roam in small herds, searching for bare spots upon which to feed.

As the day progressed, the sun rose higher above us, warming the earth and melting ice from the trees. Around eleven we crossed paths with two men riding north. Neither had seen the likes of Granger, so we thanked them and continued.

As Tom and I had talked earlier, Granger wanted both of us, and on his terms. We both believed he'd leave us some kind of word or sign. We just weren't sure what to look for. Usually, the men we hunted were not wishing to be caught, and the trail they left was always the same. This time it was different, and because Granger was the kind of man he was, I worried what he might do.

Salida had one saloon and that's where we headed first. Stopping out front, we hitched the horses then walked in, mindful of what might be waiting.

The bar room was small with a big potbelly stove in the middle of the floor. We felt its heat the moment we walked through the door. Three men stood at the bar and two others sat at a table to the right of the stove, and as we crossed to the bar their eyes followed us.

The tender was a short, skinny fellow with thick glasses that made his eyes look four times larger than they were. Tom and I each ordered a beer then looked around. Near the door where we had come in was a big, fancy stained-glass window that didn't fit the rest of the decor. The walls were rough cut boards, aged with time and the floor bore a lot of worn hollowed spots. The bar itself had been a classy one in its time, but now its polish was gone and there were dull, bare spots where the arms of drinking cowboys had leaned.

When the skinny tender came back with our beer, I handed him the sketch of Granger. Taking it he pulled the paper close to his eyes for a look.

"We're searching for this man," I said, "Have you seen him?"

After a short stare he handed it back.

"Yeah, he was here."

"When?"

"Three days I reckon." The tender paused and bit at his lower lip as if trying to remember something. Then he said, "Hey, your names don't happen to be Wade and Steinburgler, do they?"

Looking at Tom, I rolled my eyes, ignoring the big grin.

It's Wade and Steinberge," I said with irritation in my tone. The tender flushed. "Sorry."

I told him it was all right and he went on.

"This fellow was here sure enough," the man continued, "left a message for you. Said if you passed through, to tell you he hoped you felt better. Said he had something for you, over at the funeral parlor. You're to go there and talk to the undertaker. He's got some kind of instruction for ya." The skinny, large eyed man shrugged his shoulders. "Far as I can remember, that's about all."

After downing the rest of my beer, I folded the sketch and put it back in my pocket. As we turned to leave, I laid our money on the bar and headed for the door. The tender called out after us.

"Hey, if you catch up with this fella', best be careful, he's got Demons in him."

Pausing with my hand on the doorknob, I looked back, "Were there any other men with him?"

"Yep. Three."

After thanking him we walked out into the cold street.

The sky above was clear, but to the north darkness was gathering, displaying the potential for snow or rain; it looked gloomy, and inside I thought just how well it was going to fit with whatever was waiting for us at the undertakers.

His place was at the end of the street on the opposite side. When we walked in, a little bell over the door rang out, letting him know he had company. At the far end of the room in which we stood; a thick, black curtain blocked the entrance to an adjacent area. It wasn't thirty seconds when those same curtains opened and a fat, big nosed man dressed in black, walked in.

I wasted no time.

"Wade and Steinberge, we understand you have something for us?"

"And instructions, too." Tom added.

The undertaker nodded and gestured with his hand, "If you will follow me."

He led us through the black curtain into the next room. It was large; and on the walls hung all of the obvious tools of his trade: tubing, knives, pans, ropes, buckets, saws, drills and Lord only knew what else. Against one wall, eight coffins stood on end and the entire room smelled of death. I didn't like it here and it made me feel uneasy. Then we stepped into another room, this one much smaller. At the end of it a single coffin sat on two sawhorses. That's where he led us. Stopping beside it he looked from me to Tom, "It's going to smell a bit, gentlemen. The man's been waiting for you near three days." Turning, he raised the lid.

Inside lay the body of a young man no older than twenty-three or four. He was dressed in new clothing and looked peaceful. Our faces obviously showed puzzlement. Then the undertaker lifted the chin of the dead man… his throat has been cut.

Shaking my head, I looked at Tom, "That son of a bitch."

The undertaker turned to face us.

"I was instructed not to sew up the throat until I'd shown you. He said you'd know what it meant."

"What about instructions?" I asked.

"You are to go to Durango. Said there's another surprise waiting."

Tom motioned toward the coffin.

"Who was he?"

The undertaker glanced at the rough wooden box then back to us.

"Most unfortunate, this young man was our new Sheriff. I was going to bury him with his badge but the fellow you're following kept it. Said it was the proper thing. He's the one who bought him those new clothes I'm burying him in. I do admire a man who is not afraid to spend money."

The fat undertaker started to grin, but I stopped him. Grabbing the front of his suit, I pulled him to me and asked through clenched teeth.

"This fellow we're following for, did he bring you the body?"

The undertaker was shocked.

"Why…yes, said he found him like this, still had blood on his hands where he tried to help the poor soul." He frowned causing his eyebrows to touch. "Hey," he added, "you're not thinking this fellow killed our Sheriff, are you?"

"Maybe," I said.

Now his frown turned into a dumb expression. "Surely, you're mistaken, Mr. Steinberge. Why would a U.S. Marshal kill another lawman?"

Without realizing it, I tightened my grip.

"What the hell do you mean, a U.S. Marshal?"

His face went white with fear, and he began to choke.

"Please, Mister, all I know is he was wearing a badge that read United States Marshal, I just assumed, that's all."

The word came out before I could stop it. "Shit." Turning him loose I sighed, then glanced one last time at the dead man lying in the coffin. He was so young, naive; probably never saw it coming. After apologizing Tom and I left. The cold winter air felt good; it cooled the blood boiling in my veins.

Before leaving town, we checked again at the saloon. Maybe someone had witnessed the murder of the young Sheriff. But all we got was a repeat of the same story; that the U.S. Marshal had found him like that. Curious, I asked the bartender what he meant earlier about Granger having Demons in him.

"In my business, mister, you learn people. It's in their eyes…the meanness. And this man had the stare of evil. When you catch him, you better have the Lord on your side, because he's got the Devil on his."

We left Salida with the darkened sky closer; and like its gray brooding coldness, anger worse than ever filled the inside of me. Up till now, this 'game' that Granger was playing had only involved Tom and me. But now, he was involving innocent players-murdering them in cold blood. And I knew things would get worse before the end came, and that end could not come soon enough. On top of that, this bastard was wearing my badge and posing as a U.S. Marshal.

To the people of Salida that's exactly what they believed; how could they know.

To them he was the fellow lawman who had found their Sheriff and tried to save him. In all their ignorance, though it be innocent, they had no way of knowing. what a cold-blooded butcher he truly was.

For a good while Tom and I rode in silence. By the time the sun dropped behind the horizon, a cold wind had picked up and we knew a freezing night of killing temperatures lay ahead.

For me it would be a restless night; sleep would not come easy. I wanted Granger. I wanted the barrel of my colt stuck in his mouth and hear the hammer click as I pulled it back…and mostly, I wanted to feel the kick when I pulled the trigger.

CHAPTER NINE

Around 6:00 p.m., the snow began. Fastening the top button of my coat, I looked up into the sky and watched the steady fall of flakes. Tom was doing the same.

In an attempt at ignoring the bitter cold our conversation focused on good times and good things. Tom had mentioned a ranch near by; Tom said he knew the family and was sure they would put us up for the night.

By dark the wind grew worse, and snow began drifting. Turning my back to the wind I rolled a cigarette, lighting it with a cupped hand. Although small, the warmth felt good, and a cup of hot-coffee, or flask of bourbon would have added nicely to my liking. Tom talked about Caroline and the children for some time; smiling over things they had shared and hoped for. His son had wanted to grow up and become a Texas Ranger and track down outlaws like his dad and Uncle Archy; that's what the boy called me. As for his daughter, her ambition had been to grow up and be a teacher…getting married was out of the question though, since boys were icky and silly. Caroline had wanted two more children to complete the family, another boy and girl. Her dream for Tom was to get out of law enforcement and into a safer profession. Maybe open a store or some such thing since he had experience. Her most heartfelt desire though, Tom had said sheepishly, was that he attend a seminary, and become a pastor.

Tom talked on for a long while, and as he talked, I was more than happy to listen. They say talking about a difficult time is good medicine; that it's a sign a person is coming to grips with the problem he faces. Tom Wade was my closet friend and I wanted nothing more than to be there for him.

We found the house around 8:30. Our finding it was part Tom's memory and part luck. The snow fall had turned into a blizzard, and it was by chance we strolled right into the yard.

His friends seemed happy for the company. After bedding down the horses in the barn, we went into the house where we received a heartfelt welcome with lots of smiles and handshakes. They were the McKinnen family; John and Marilyn, both our age, in their forties, two boys, thirteen and sixteen, and a white-headed grandfather who smoked a pipe with good smelling tobacco.

Marilyn cooked us ham and eggs and warmed up some coffee. The house was cozy, and I was glad to be there. While we ate, Tom and John relived their Army days. Both had served with Sherman, and both had been wounded at Gettysburg. I had noticed John limping when we came in and now, I knew why.

When Tom told them about Caroline and the children there was crying and sympathy that came from the heart. And from that point on they made sure the conversation didn't come up again.

We talked and laughed and shared past experiences for hours. When the boys were finally ordered to bed, they protested but obeyed respectfully. Upon bidding their good nights they both made it a point to shake our hands and invite us back. I admired the McKinnens, and after seeing their close family ties understood even more clearly now, Tom's personal loss.

When we ourselves finally called it a night, Tom and I rose and headed for our coats at the door. We were going to the barn to turn in, but John, Marilyn and even Grandpa blocked the doorway. So, unable to refuse we rolled out our bed roles near the fire and settled for the night.

As the warmth of the fire laid way for the easing in of sleep, my mind reflected once again upon the McKinnens. They had cheerfully fed us, put us up for the night and shared much of their personal life. I recalled too the politeness of their children. Tom was truly fortunate to call them friends; and now I was happy to say they were mine too.

Outside, wind howled at the door and windows, but it was of little concern, for inside there was warmth, the warmth of the fire and the warmth of friends. And warm too was the sleep that came and gave rest to my tired bones.

*

A surprise was waiting for us in Durango; that's what the undertaker had said. Riding into town uneasiness sat heavy in the pit of my stomach. Granger wasn't just crazy he was sick, insanely sick; so, there was no telling what we'd find.

The town was busy with early afternoon activity. Streets were full of wagons and single riders. The walkways clambered with people and nearly all the hitching posts were full.

At the hotel we had to do some fast talking to get a room. It turned out a case of right place at the right time. A gentleman had cancelled out and it came down to giving the only room to one of two parties, Tom and I, or a fancy dressed reporter from a large Chicago newspaper. Much to the angry disappointment of the newspaperman, I was more convincing. With a red face he stormed out, but not before calling us a couple of gun-slinging outlaws who delighted in pushing innocent citizens around. Grinning at Tom, I told him it was probably his glasses and shaggy beard.

Our room number was sixteen. It overlooked the street and I liked that since we were expecting a surprise. After shedding our gear, we both rented baths and cleaned up. I shaved then running a hand over my smooth face, explained to Tom how great it felt. He threw a wet towel at me and said the newspaperman had been right.

Feeling cleaner we strapped on our guns then went out for something to eat. Finding a little restaurant a few doors down we went in and ordered steak. While waiting, we sipped coffee and talked.

"You know," I told Tom, "When Granger beat up on me outside of Leadville, he had two men with him. In Salida there were three."

Tom nodded. "Yeah, I know. Truthfully, it concerns me just a little. He seems to be collecting them and I wonder what's he up to?"

I took a sip of coffee then put the cup back on the saucer.

"I don't know. But I don't like it. And it concerns me too. We don't need any more people killed over this situation. We must catch him and do it fast."

Tom cut in. "He's no fool Arch. I mean, here we are in Durango because that's the way 'he' wants it. So far, he has called all the shots and we've done all the beckoning. Somehow, we've got to turn that around."

"You're right. And maybe the answer lies here in Durango."

Tom took a sip from his cup, and I turned to stare out the window. The town was too busy; something was going on, something out of the ordinary. I'd been to Durango before and had never seen this much activity.

The waiter arriving pulled my attention back. He served Tom first and while he was setting the plate in front of him, I asked. "What's all the commotion in town?"

He looked at me like I was ignorant. "You mean you haven't heard?"

"Heard what?"

"There's a rumor of an Indian uprising again. Folks have been pouring into town for three days now. They say the Utes killed a farm family north of here; butchered them right good. Took their scalps they did."

Tom grabbed the waiter's arm. "What was the name of the family?"

Not pleased, the waiter looked down at Tom's hand and he let go.

"The name," Tom repeated, "I asked you the name."

The waiter stared down at him as if holding the answer intentionally, liking the feel of it. Then he cleared his throat and blurted it out. "Porter. Okay?" The waiter spun around on his heels then and was gone.

Tom sighed and I followed suit. "I'm as thankful and relieved as you are Tom." I told him. "But you know what this means don't you?"

"No. What?"

"It means we don't have a chance at all of getting a refill on our coffee."

CHAPTER TEN

After we'd finished eating, I paid the bill and we walked to the nearest saloon. I wanted a word with the Sheriff but figured it best Tom didn't come along; there was no need in agitating an already impossible situation. Our plan was simple: we'd ask a few questions at the bar, then while Tom waited there, I'd go over to the Sheriff's office.

When we walked into the saloon, I counted eight men, two at the bar and the others sitting around tables. We ordered a beer and when the tender set them in front of us he asked.

"You boys heard about the uprising? They say it's going to be a bad one; even heard Geronimo himself was headed up this way." I started to pull Granger's sketch out of my pocket when the bartender added, "even heard we've got a killer headed this way. An outlaw they call Cold Blood Wade, wanted for the murder of four men. Killed them in cold blood he did. Hell, half the men in town are on the lookout for him. Guess there's a big reward, dead or alive."

Unfolding the sketch of Granger, I handed it to the tender. "Have you seen this man?"

"Sure. He's the Marshal from Denver. He's the one who warned us about this fellow Wade."

"When was he here?"

"Let's see." The tender began. "This is Friday. I think it was Tuesday; or there about."

Not to look suspicious, Tom and I finished our beer then left cautiously together. We figured it would no longer be wise to keep with our original plan. His hanging around the saloon suddenly seemed a bad idea; the seclusion of the hotel room would be better.

While he waited there, I visited the Sheriff's Office. The man behind the desk was Carl Stone. I knew him only causally, but at least he was a follow lawman I trusted. Handing him the drawing of Granger, I asked if he had seen him. He paused a bit before handing it back.

"Sure did. A couple of days ago; didn't stay long, just passing through."

"Know anything about him?"

"No. Not really." Stone drummed the top of his desk with his fingers and added, "There was one thing."

"What's that?" I asked.

"The man wore a Marshal's Badge…from Denver. It just didn't fit. I know most of the men who wear them, or get some kind of notification about them, but I knew nothing of him." Stone paused, and added, "What's your beef with this fellow anyway?"

I explained the whole story and he listened intently. It felt good confiding in another lawman. The way things were stacking up I figured it might prove worthwhile to start building a network of dependable cooperates.

When I left, we shook hands, and he offered his help anytime. He said to give Tom his best and advised me to keep him in the hotel room out of sight. I did just that; we remained there the rest of the evening. It was agreed we'd pull out in the morning under the cover of darkness, so by ten we were in bed with the lantern low. For a long while I lay awake mulling over all that had been happening. Before falling asleep Tom had asked a question that left me wondering and remaining awake. He had asked if I thought there might be a connection between Granger and the uprising.

With a sigh I rested my hands behind my head. The surprise we were expecting obviously had been the alerting of the town to Tom's coming. But, thanks to his change in looks, Granger's plan failed for no one had recognized him.

Tom's breathing was easy and shallow. He was sleeping peacefully. Closing my eyes, I ordered all thoughts out of my head and yawned. Like Tom, sleep was what I wanted, needed and…that was the last thing I remembered before the banging on the door woke me. Tom and I rolled off the bed together grabbing our guns. The voice behind the door was Stone.

"Steinberge, let me in. It's important."

Sleep still fogging my mind I turned up the lantern wondering what he could possibly want at this hour. My pocket-watch read, 3:02 a.m.

Unlocking the door, I let him in; behind him followed two deputies. Once inside I closed the door then Tom and I holstered our guns. That was when they pulled theirs.

At first, I couldn't figure out what was going on. Then it dawned. Stone pulled back the hammer of his pistol and grinned. "I've come for him." He glanced at Tom then back to me. I knew there was anger in my face.

"What the hell are you talking about, Stone? I explained all that. He's my prisoner and in my custody until I personally return him to Denver."

"Not in my town." He spoke. "In my town, we do things my way, the Stone way."

I wanted to go for him, to grab him by the throat, but there were too many. Now was not the time.

The two deputies went around to the side of the bed where Tom stood and put chains on his wrists; they jingled loudly in the early morning stillness. My eyes were as cold as the wind beyond the window, and I looked straight into Stone's face.

"I trusted you. You're a fellow lawman. Were a fellow lawman, now you're a son of a bitch."

He laughed. "You don't know when you're beat do you, Steinberge?"

Then they were gone…and Tom Wade was out of my protection. How could I have been stupid enough to trust anyone? Even a Sheriff.

With hands that shook from anger, I rolled a cigarette. What I wanted to do was march straight over to the jail and break Carl Stone's neck. Who in the hell did he think he was? And what did he mean by my not knowing when I was beat?

I finished the smoke while pacing the floor, trying to think things out calmly. Storming straight over to Stone's office and flat taking Tom back was what I really wanted to too, and Stone or his deputies wouldn't stop me. But that was not the answer, there was a better way.

Taking one last draw, I threw the butt down and crushed it out with my foot, realizing I didn't have my boots on. The butt was hot, but not as hot as me. Looking over at Tom's side of the bed I saw his boots sitting there too and realized they had taken him out in his stocking feet. His coat still hung on the rack as well. The bastards hadn't even given him time to finish dressing for the cold.

Strapping on my gun and pulling on my boots, I grabbed my coat and hat then went out the door. For the time being I'd go along with doing things the Stone way, however, the tide was about to change.

Leaving the hotel, I stepped out into the cold morning air. Immediately I saw my breath but didn't care. Turning right, I hurried down the plank walkway listening to the click of my boot heels in the quiet morning. The streets were empty and even the saloons were closed.

The building I wanted sat at the end of the street. I had seen it when we rode in, and despite the fact I knew what I'd find when I reached it, it didn't matter. What needed to be done was important, and perhaps for Tom, a matter of life or death.

When I stepped in front of the Telegraph Office the building was as dark as the sky. In the back, however, was a small residence and I was willing to bet the operator hung his hat there. Cutting through the alley, I went around to the door and started pounding. I really hated to bother him at this hour, but this was too important to wait.

The dim light of a lantern moved slowly toward the door where I stood, and the voice of an old man asked me what the hell I thought I was doing.

"I'm sorry, but I have to send some telegrams."

"Now?"

"Yes now. It's a matter of life or death."

I listened as the old man fumbled with the lock and let me in. With him leading the way, we maneuvered through the small house out into the telegraph office.

Grumbling to himself, he put down the lantern and sat at his desk. Looking up he said. "All right sonny, let's have it."

Pulling up a chair, I sat beside him.

"To the Governor State of Colorado.

Need help. Can't explain. Order Sheriff of Durango to release prisoner Tom Wade to me.

Do immediately.

Signed: A. Steinberge. U.S. Marshal."

The old man clicked it off then grumbled. "Next."

"To John Evens. Denver. John. Need pull.

Talk to Governor. Tell release Tom Wade to me.

Will explain another time. Thanks. Signed: A. Steinberge.

Again, the handset clicked away. When he had finished the old fellow looked over at me. "That it?"

"One more."

He signed and shook his head. "Have at it. But mind you, my fingers are getting sore."

"To Lt. Governor Tabor. State of Colorado.

Horace. Convince boss. Release Tom Wade to me.

Thanks. Signed A. Steinberge."

When he was finished this time, the old man sat back and sighed. "Now are we done?"

Patting his shoulder, I stood up.

"Yes." I told him smiling. "And send the bill to the Sheriff's Office here in Durango; to Carl Stone."

He looked up at me with a funny expression, not quite sure of the order. Then he said. "Well, I reckon you know what you're talking about. You seem to know some important folks. I'll do that."

Taking out a five-dollar piece, I handed it to him and winked. "Here, for your trouble."

CHAPTER ELEVEN

Returning to the hotel, I gathered Tom's boots, hat and coat. The jail would be cold, and he would need them. The telegrams I sent would undoubtedly do the trick, but it was not the way I preferred to handle it. What I really wanted to do was take Tom back and hope Stone tried to stop me. Men like him were a disgrace to the star.

When I walked into the Sheriff's Office, a lone lantern suspended from the ceiling provided the only light. It had been turned down low and the room was covered in dark shadows. The jail looked deserted. I didn't like it. Easing the colt out of its holster, I set Tom's things down on Stone's desk and scanned the room. At the back, the door leading into the cell area was partially ajar.

Listening carefully, I could detect no sound. So cautiously I made my way to the doorway and paused. Still, I heard nothing. Waiting for my eyes to adjust to the added darkness inside the cell area, my mind ran through ideas of what might be going on. Then, in one swift easy movement, I was inside kneeling beside an empty cell, gun ready. Nothing happened. There was no one here.

Where was Tom? About the time I rose to my feet the door outside opened and someone came into the office. Turning quickly, I glanced out into the lighted area. It was one of the deputies who'd come for Tom. I had to move fast; it would be a matter of seconds before he noticed Tom's things sitting on the desk.

Kicking open the door I stepped out into the light with gun pointed.

"Go for that gun and I'll shoot off your saddle horn then turn you around and put another hole in your ass."

Surprised, he spun around. Slowly his hands went into the air. Moving closer, I put on a mean face, one I wanted him to see. "I'll ask you one time, then things get rough. The choice is yours."

His face twisted into a look of uncertainty, but I knew he would not be easy to scare.

"Where is Wade?"

He grinned. "Go shit in your saddle."

"Aren't we funny." I told him. When I brought the butt of the colt down across his face, blood flew. So did he, straight back against the wall then down onto the floor in a sitting position. He grabbed at his face and swore.

I didn't relent. "Get up Mr. Funny man." I said, "This is where it gets rough like I promised."

He scrambled to his feet holding his face. Blood seeped through his fingers. I would have preferred he just told me. but men like him must be convinced. Stepping in closer I said, "Now, one more time, where is Wade?"

He made a lunge for me, but I was ready. Side stepping, I let him go by cracking his head with the gun barrel this time. To the floor he went, moaning. Being the nice guy, I can be when I must, I helped him to his feet. After holstering the pistol, I shoved him against the wall, a hand to his throat.

"This is the last chance. You don't tell me what I want, I'll kill you right here."

"All right, all right, he's with Stone and Gifford, on their way to Tucson."

"I don't know, I just do what I'm told around here."

I tightened my grip and his eyes bulged.

"Why Tucson?"

"Okay." He was barely able to speak. I lightened my grip. "They're taking him to Granger."

"Good cowboy." I said, "Now tell me about their location in Tucson."

"The Booker Ranch. A big spread north of the city."

"Why the Booker Ranch?"

His face was covered in blood now. "Damn mister, go easy, I'm bleeding to death."

Again, I tightened my grasp, and he squeaked out the words. "Charles Booker is Grange's half-brother. They have some kind of business deal going."

Things were beginning to make sense now.

"What kind of business?"

"Honest to God mister, I don't know. You'd have to ask Stone."

"One more question than you can go see the Doc."

There was pleading in his voice.

"Damn it, what?"

"What direction are they headed?"

"West. Toward the Mancos River."

I let go of him and he slid down the wall to the floor. Gathering Tom's things, I ambled to the door then stopped and turned to face him.

"If you're lying to me and I don't find Tom Wade, I'm coming back, and you won't need a doctor."

I walked out, leaving the door open behind me. The air was cold, but the sky was full of stars. For that I was thankful. They wouldn't be that far ahead, half an hour maybe. Hurrying to the stable, I saddled up Gertrude and rode out.

Following their trail was no chore thanks to the snow and light of the stars. For the first mile or so there were three sets of tracks. Then one of them turned away and angled back toward town. I wasn't sure who, probably Stone.

When the depth of the snow allowed, I put Gertrude into full gallop. I wanted to cover as much ground as quickly as possible. There was no telling Tom's condition. I had his coat, boots and hat with me. Maybe they had given him one of theirs, but I doubted it.

I wondered how men like Stone became the law. His kind belonged behind bars, not a badge. And what was he doing in a friendship with Granger, why would he, a Sheriff in a town the size of Durango, be so influenced by the likes of such a cruel and heartless man? What did Granger have over Stone? Was it money? And just what caliber of man was Granger's lawmen. They were owned lawmen! Sighing, I looked up into the stars. Whatever caliber it was, I intended to find out; but first I needed to get to Tom.

Far off in the distance at what seemed to be the very end of the earth, the very tip of the sun peeked over the horizon. The stars and darkness were quickly fading. Somewhere ahead, Tom and the lone rider traveled on, hopefully not suspecting that I was following. By now Stone was back in town conversing with his doctored deputy. I didn't care. Even if they rode back out, I'd have Tom back before they reached us.

We were halfway between Durango and the river when I spotted them. Kicking Gertrude in the ribs, she broke into a full gallop. There could be no other way. They were a long distance off. Maybe the deputy would think I was Stone returning before he caught on. It worked. I was on top of him before he realized what happened.

He thought about going for his gun, but my pulled colt changed his mind. I ordered him to drop his pistol in the snow and he obeyed.

With the barrel of mine, I motioned toward Tom. His hands were still chained behind him and as I had suspected, he was without a coat and boots.

"Unchain him, and when you're done try something stupid, I'd like that."

Aside from throwing me a dirty look, he did as he was told.

Once freed, Tom worked his wrists while I dug out his belongings. When I threw them to him, he smiled. "Thanks partner."

"No problem." My eyes went back to the deputy. "Get down off the horse. It's time for a walk."

His eyes filled with surprise. "You must be kidding. "It's a long way back into town, and it's freezing out here."

Not showing any emotion I shrugged. "No, I'm not kidding. Now get your worthless butt down or I'll knock you out of the saddle, and if you turn your horse and run, I'll shoot you down like the dog you are."

Reluctantly, he dismounted then looked at me with hate on his face. I gave him the same look back and told him to give me his coat.

Tom cut in. "No Arch. Let him keep it. We'll take the horse but not his coat."

He looked up at Tom with surprised eyes, "What's the matter," I asked, "Forget what it's like to be shown kindness?"

At that I grabbed the reins of his mount. We turned east...headed back to Durango.

CHAPTER TWELVE

Just shy of an hour we were back in the hotel room. We rode in the back way and entered the hotel through the rear entrance; the less conspicuous the better. Our horses were tied in the alley out of sight, and now it was but a matter of waiting. Stone's office looked deserted, but we figured both he and his deputy were in town somewhere.

From our window we could barely see the front of his office, but it was enough to observe who went in and who came out. Pulling a chair to the window I sat and rolled a smoke. The taste of the tobacco relaxed me. Blowing a small ring toward the ceiling I told Tom.

"That was a nice thing you did for the deputy out there. He didn't deserve it."

Tom was sitting on the edge of bed; rising he came over to the window and looked past me down into the street.

"I know, Arch."   He said matter of fact. "But they say whatever a man does, it comes back to him, and I believe it, you do good you get good, you do bad and bad comes back to you. It's that simple." He patted my shoulder then and returned to the bed and stretched out.

I took another draw from the cigarette giving thought to his words. My mind flashed back to Stone's office-to the deputy I'd beaten up on. Would that come back to me? It could, but then again maybe it had already, in the trashing I'd taken from Granger. And what of the other deputy; I had made him walk back to town without his horse, while he had made Tom ride out without his coat. Wasn't that coming back to him? I know the good Lord has a way of keeping everything in balance, if I had learned nothing else in my 40 years of hard living, I had learned that.

A movement caught my eye. Stone was back. I watched him stroll into his office beside the deputy I had struck with my pistol. There was a bandage on the deputy's face, and I was willing to bet Al Steinberge wasn't his favorite person. The other deputy taking the morning walk wouldn't be in for some time yet, so I was sure Stone had no idea we were even around. And I didn't want him to know-at least not yet anyway. Not until the telegram arrived. When it did, I would march it over to his office and stress one very important thing...that things were not always done the Stone way, in his town. Too, I had a lot of questions for the Sheriff of Durango. Like whom was Charles Booker? His deputy had said he was a half-brother to Ganger, but what was their story and what were they up to? And what was this business deal mentioned? And what was Stone's connection to all of it?

At noon Tom took over at the window and I went down to the lobby were I ordered sandwiches. Then using the back door again slipped out into the alley and worked my way down to the street to the telegraph office. The same door I used the night before was unlocked so I entered that way. No one else was around and the old man recognized me immediately.

"Reckon I know what you're looking' for he said eyes fixed." Pulling open a desk drawer he lifted out an envelope and handed it to me with a grin. "I didn't tell nary a soul, I wanted to mind you. But I forced myself to keep my trap shot. I've never known anybody as important as the likes of you. Those are some pretty important fellows you know. You must be some kind of a big shot."

Grinning, I took it from his hand. "My friend," I told him opening the envelope, "If this says what I think it will, you just may have saved a man's life, and that will make you the big shot."

He watched with anxious eyes.

With the gram open I read aloud so he could hear.

To: Town of Durango Sheriff
`You are ordered immediately to
release prisoner, Tom Wade to
Marshal Steinberge
Failure to do so will result in
Strong consequences.
Signed: Tabor, A. W. Lt. Governor
State of Colorado.

When I folded it up and stuck it back in the envelope the old man pulled out a second gram.

"This one came to young fellow, right after that one."

Taking it from his hand I opened it and read aloud, again, knowing it would make the old man feel important.

To: Al Steinberge U.S. Marshall.
What the hell is going on down there.
You'll have some explaining to do.
Give Tom our best. Keep us informed.
Be careful.
Signed: Horace, T.

I folded that Graham too and stuck them both in my pocket. The old man was smiling at me. I returned his smile then started toward the front door. "Hey." He called out after me. "Aren't you going out the wrong way?"

I gave him a wink. "Not this time friend."

CHAPTER THIRTEEN

Back at the hotel room, Tom and I ate our sandwiches in a hurry, we were both anxious to visit Carl Stone. After signing for the hotel bill, we walked out into the street. The sun was bright, and the sky was clear. We retrieved the horses and brought them around front to a hitch. After stowing our gear, we walked side by side into Stone's office.

He was sitting behind his desk leaned back in his chair. When he saw us, his mouth opened but he didn't say anything, fear flushed his face. Sitting beside him with his feet propped up was the deputy with the bandage. He started to get up, but I told him to stay saddled. The man was a quick learner, he listened this time. Looking directly at Stone I grinned, "Surprised to see us?"

Stone tried hard to gather his composure.

"I thought..."

"Thought you'd never see us again, or that maybe your other deputy had killed me? And speaking of killing, that's why you doubled back isn't it? To see to it I never left town. Fearing Mr. Bandage Face there couldn't handle the job by himself. Well, you were right, he couldn't. You know it's just like they say, Stone. If you want the job done right, you got do-it-yourself. So here I am, get it done. Stand up!"

His face went white. The fear was wild in his eyes. I edged my voice with harshness. "I said get out of the chair."

He didn't want to, but slowly he rose to his feet, lips pressed hard together. The chair creaked as he left it, beads of perspiration were showing on his forehead. Looking straight in his eyes I told him. "When you got back to town and saw your deputy had flubbed things up, you got scared, but you figured even if I killed the deputy with Tom, we'd just ride on into Tucson anyway, not bothering to come back here, right?"

Our hands were near out guns. Eyes locked, I waited. His deputy sat glued to his chair as he stared from Stone to me. Tom had him covered so I didn't worry. Outside a wagon jingled by and people strolled past the window talking. I saw it in his eyes. He flinched then grabbed for it. My Gun was in my hand before his cleared leather. Frozen, he stood there, no idea what to do now. I widened my smile. "Ease it back in and sit like a good dog." There was anger on his face, but relief too.

Reaching into my pocket I pulled the telegrams out and threw them on his desk. "Read!"

When he picked them up his hands were shaking. I made him read out loud. He hated it and I loved it. Normally I'd never treat a man this way, stealing his dignity, but Stone was the exception, he was a Granger worshiper.

When finished I took the telegrams back and stuck them in my pocket. "Just in case you decide to gather a posse and ride after us, you remember two things: first, I have these and anyone who rides with you will have ridden into the cold for nothing, they can't touch us. If even one person sets out on our tail I will personally come back here and stick the barrow of my pistol up your ass before I pull the trigger." Stone was staring in cold contempt. "And when you wire Granger, you tell him I'm coming for him, coming for my badge, tell him to be wearing it right over his heart; that way the hole I put through the center will serve as a constant reminder I killed someone for the first time out of pure pleasure. You got that?"

Stone was beginning to feel brave. "Yeah, I got it Steinberge, and you're going to get it. Granger will kill you. You think you're tough, but he's tougher."

"Tougher than you, I hope. I'd at least like a challenge."

After locking them in their own jail I threw the keys into a half-filled chamber pot and we walked out.

Inside I felt good, like finally things might be going our way. Granger's surprise for us had done a complete turnabout. Now it was Tom and I who were calling the shots. I knew things would not be pleasant when we got to Tucson, but then I never expected they would. I did wish; however, I could see the expression on Granger's face when he received Stone's telegram.

*

The four days to Tucson were long ones. They had become days that seemed weeks. We came into Arizona just north of Round Rock, then rode down to Winslow, remaining on the desert floor. In agreement we avoided the climb up to Flagstaff, believing Granger was himself anxious to get to Tucson and would not take time out to stop there.

From Winslow we made our way across the open desert to Phoenix and down to Casa Grande. It was just south of there a few miles we made camp for the last time before taking our ride into Tucson. We were out of the snow here and the terrain was barren except for scattered sagebrush and occasional cactus. This was a brown empty land burned by too many centuries beneath a scorching sun. During the day it was hot, and at night we sat wearing coats while huddled in a blanket. Because of the Indian troubles we camped without a fire and tonight would be no different.

Tom and I missed the hot coffee, but the light of a fire was not worth announcing our presence to anyone interested in killing us. If trouble were too come our way, we preferred it happen in the light of day. For us now, there would be enemies lurking in the shadows.

Over the desert the night sky lay thick with the glitter of stars, a blanched moon stared down with eyes as gray as the night was cold and a soft wind pecked at the blankets Tom and I held wrapped around us. We felt alone, like two men huddled at the center of a world filled with muted blackness.

Tom took a draw from the cigarette I'd built for him then looked over at me.

"Think Granger will be waiting for us tomorrow?"

I shook my head. "No."

Half smiling, he replied. "Me either. He won't make it that easy."

I agreed with Tom, from here on out nothing would be easy. This was Granger country and neither of us had any idea how much influence he held in Tucson.

Somewhere in the distant darkness a coyote howled, and Gertrude raised her ears. A few seconds passed than she relaxed. Gertrude was a good judge of noises, animal or man, so when she relaxed, so did I.

Tom and I talked well into the night. The last topic of conversation, although I had no idea how it came around to that, had been the importance of patience. When he finally rolled onto his side and pulled his blanket tight around him, I looked off into the desert.

I whispered the word to myself, "patience." Tom had said something that stuck with me; a verse from a good book, he had heard a sermon on it during one of his Sunday meetings. It had, he told me warmly, been one of Caroline's favorites; one she practiced and jokingly teased him with, saying it was the secret of their happy marriage. Caroline herself, he had said, possessed the patience of a saint and had many times taught him its importance. His words rang in my head like a church bell. "In your patience possess ye your soul".

As I sat there staring into the desert, of all things, that verse made me think of Granger, realizing just how anxious I was in wanting to face him, to beat a confession out of him. And in my thoughts too, was a restless eagerness to kill him for what he did to Caroline and the children…and Tom. Yet, I knew inside, killing was not the answer. I served the law and he needed to go to trial. Sighing with uncertainty I made a face there in the moonlight. I really didn't know what I wanted. It felt as if there were two of me, one yearning to gun him down and the other wanting to drag him back to Denver for trial and hanging.

One more time the world was turning gray, giving up no clear answer. How simple it would be if I could see through the eyes of a child, to them life was simple; right is right and wrong is wrong; we all have to grow up though, and through those years of life we wear down, little by little, time whittling away at our mind and body until finally, we reach that point when we've had enough, and one day the thought of slipping away into that great eternal sleep becomes a not so bad idea.

Once again, I sighed into the gray cold-darkness of the desert. Ironic I thought. Here I sit, a tiny speck of a man huddled beneath his wool blanket in the middle of this barren and near-lightless world, realizing for the first time that without patience, a man's life lacks substance, he becomes a reckless being, charging through life and missing out on so many of the little things that often mean so much. And too, in lacking patients, especially in the West, death quite often comes prematurely.

The prayer verse Tom had quoted said a man processes his soul through patients, that was important too, because when the time came for me to die, be it by God's own hand, old age or a bullet, I'd want my soul going up and not down. Heaven would be like the great Rocky Mountains of Colorado in all its beauty and splendor. Hell, on the other hand, would be a Death Valley; a land filled with burning heat and empty nothingness; and worse, Hell would be filled with men like Granger.

Pulling the blanket tight around me, I laid down, pillowing my head against the saddle. The wind was picking up. With gun in hand I closed my eyes and smiled at what I saw... a 16 once steak, medium rare with a baked Potato on the side. My stomach growled and that was last thing I remembered.

CHAPTER FOURTEEN

We rode into Tucson beneath a bright afternoon sun. The streets were busy, but unlike Durango, they were busy with the towns everyday affairs. After boarding the horses at the livery, we walked up the street to the hotel. It would feel good to sleep in a bed again. The clerk behind the desk received us in warm manner. He was a short, stocking man with a thin mustache that traced along the edge of his upper lip. His hair was curly black, and he wore a wide brimmed visor with matching arm and band.

"Well, welcome gents. It's always nice to see new faces. Just passing through?"

I shrugged and put on a big smile. "Don't know for sure. We're looking for a friend of ours and if he's here we won't have a choice. He'll make us stay and won't let us leave until we're so drunk, they'll lock us all up."

The clerk smiled back. "Sounds like you're in for quite a time. What's your friends name, maybe I know him."

I handed Tom the pen so he could sign the register, then told the clerk.

"Granger, do you know him?"

There was no hesitation. "Golly yes, he's related to Mr. Booker. More than likely that's where he is right now."

"Great." I said, "Then I have just two more questions?"

"Sure, Mr..."

The clerk glanced quickly at the register then back at me. "Steinberge."

I gave him another smile. "Who is Mr. Booker and where exactly does he live?"

The clerk looked shocked. "Golly, if you know Mr. Granger, I'm really surprised you haven't heard him talk about Mr. Booker; he's only the biggest rancher around...and the richest to! Carries a lot of weight in this town, in the whole state for that matter. And wait until you meet Mr. Booker's sister. She's quite a looker." His face went red, as if he had said something wrong, then he added quickly. "But she's a lady, yes sir, a fine lady too." Pausing thoughtfully, he looked down at the counter. "Let's see, what else did you want to know...oh yes, how to get to Mr. Booker's ranch. Heck, you may have passed it if you came in from the North. Just ride straight out of town on the main road for about three miles, there you'll come to a fork, turn left, go one more mile and you'll see the ranch. Can't miss it, it's BIG."

We thanked him and asked that he not tell Granger he saw us. "No sir," he said handing us our key. "My lips are sealed. I wouldn't want to be the one to spoil his surprise." Giving one last nod we turned and mounted the stairs. He put us in room 13 and I hoped that wasn't an omen of things to come.

The room was clean but typical: one double bed, dresser with bowl and pitcher, a lantern, chamber pot and window overlooking the alley. Much to my dissatisfaction the door did not have a lock.

After washing up we returned to the lobby and asked the clerk for the name of a good restaurant. "There are two." He told us. "The fanciest would be the Steer House, that's where all the big people go."

"By big people, you mean people like those who overeat." I said kiddingly.

He didn't know quite how to take my humor and cleared his throat, "No sir, I mean big like famous."

Waving my hand in apology, I told him. "I know. I was just kidding."

He pondered for a second then smiled, glad I cleared things up. Tom smiled to, shaking his head at me. Meanwhile the clerk continued. "The other place in town is called the Trails Restaurant. That's where all the small people go." He broke with a burst of laughter and looked from Tom to me, waiting for us to catch his humor, so out of courtesy we laughed. He was still laughing when we turned to leave.

Out on the street the sun was bright. Showing a slight grin Tom commented. "You really had that fellow rolling in there. Maybe you ought to get out of the Marshalling business and into theatrics."

"Great advice; Mr. Franklin look alike."

We chose the Steer House. It had been a while since we had had a good meal and we wanted the best. Just as the clerk said, the place was nice and had a touch of class. The tables were draped with white linen clothes and matching rolled napkins. On the walls, a soft pink rose pattern paper ran from the ceiling down to about three feet from the floor where it had been wainscoted in beautiful knotty pine. The floor itself shined brightly, and gentle lantern light set the mood for a relaxing atmosphere.

We chose a table in the far corner so we could keep our backs to a wall and watch the front door.

The kitchen was nearby, and we could hear mumbled voices mixed with the faint rattle of dishes. Tom and I had been seated only a few seconds when the waiter came over with menus; he was quite a novelty.

The man was young, probably mid '20s, with long, blond hair pony-tailed in the back with a pink ribbon. When he walked, we couldn't help noticing the distinct sway of his shoulders, or the way he kept his left arm bent at the elbow and hand flexed. He was dressed in white linen pants and a shirt as pink as the flowers on the wall; an earring dangled from his left ear...and it was pink to.

All the while he took our orders he kept his eyes on me, smiling, and wetting his lips with his tongue. Hell, I doubted he even saw Tom sitting opposite me...who seemed to be having the time of his life watching it all.

When the order was written he thanked us, gave me a wink then walked away. As soon as he was gone Tom leaned across the table and wiggled his eyebrows at me. "Archibald Steinberge." He said grinning. "I'm so jealous."

"Shut up Franklin," I told him, "Or otherwise go for your gun."

Tom had ordered liver and onions with fried potatoes and a piece of Apple pie. I ordered a 16-once steak, baked potato, sliced tomatoes, role and chocolate cake. Both of us ordered coffee.

While we waited a few people came and went, most were couples, but no one we would have passed as a Mr. Booker. Twice during our meal, the waiter came by to refill our coffee cup and smile at me.

And all the while we ate, I took notice of one very important fact; when people rose to leave, it was the waiter, the smiling man in pink who manned the cash register. When it came time to leave, I made Tom pay the bill.

CHAPTER FIFTEEN

For the time being we avoided saloons. While in Tucson, where Ganger had friends of unknown numbers the want for a drink could present us with trouble we didn't need.

Besides, we knew where Booker lived so that was enough to satisfy us... at least for now.

Walking into the lobby the clerk smiled sheepishly and asked which restaurant we had chosen. When we told him the steer house, his smile widened and he asked me "And what did you think of the waiter, Mr. Steinberge?" Looking at him, I smiled back , "A very nice boy. In fact, I thought I saw a resemblance. Is he your son?" The big smile on the clerk's ' face disappeared and so did he.

Back at the room we took off our boots and made ourselves at home.

I placed a chair under the door handle to serve as a lock just in case an unwanted visitor should try to walk in. Except for supper later, we remained behind the locked door.

As darkness crept its way into the streets, people began thinning, until finally the air wa hardly tolerable and there was no one left at all. Around eleven, we blew out the lantern and closed our eyes.

The hotel was quiet and outside there were no sounds to be heard.

The bed was soft, and sleep came quickly for the both of us.

As I slept, I dreamt. My heartbeat quickened and sweat broke out on my forehead. I wakened to find Tom missing. In worry and panic, I raced out of the hotel and into the darkened street below. It was deserted. I screamed for Tom and begged for him to answer me, but I was alone. In fear for him, I began running through the streets and into buildings, searching. My pace became frantic. Tears stung my eyes and I found myself yelling into the dark, empty night.

"Where is he? Give him back. Granger, don't you hurt him, don't cut him. Then, Granger himself appeared suddenly in the street just in front of me; his hand was on his gun, and he was laughing. Tears streaming my face I demanded he tell me where Tom was, but he laughed all the harder. Enraged with anger my hand went for my gun, but the holster was empty, then in the blink of an eye, the street around me was lined with hundreds of people. Men, women and children... all chanting the words: show him, show him, show him... and their chanting grew louder and louder until it hurt my ears and I covered them with my hands.

I wanted to turn and run, but there was no place I could go for the crowd had gathered in a huge circle around me and I was trapped in the center with Granger and his insane laughter.

The sound of their voices was deafening and as I held my ears, I began to stagger, whispering Tom's name under my breath.

Then Granger raised his hand in the air and there was immediate silence. To my left the crowd opened, exposing the door leading into the stable. It was half ajar but I could not see in. As I removed my hands from my ears, I looked into their faces. They were smiling, all of them, and I knew what they wanted. I was to enter the barn, but I yelled at them... NO! and they harmonized back, YES! Then the circle of smiling bodies began closing in on me, forcing me closer to the door... and I screamed to God to please not make me.

Then my hand was on the latch and the crowd was pressed against me... suddenly I was inside. Light was everywhere. As my eyes made the adjustment from dark to bright, I wiped away tears with the sleeve of my shirt. Silence, like the eerie state of death, loomed supreme... except for a frighteningly familiar sound coming from a semi darkened stall at the far end of the stable. It gripped me with terror- for many times I had presided at a hanging, and only too well did I recognize the noise of a lifeless body swaying at the end of a stretched rope.

Trembling, I moved closer to the sound, my legs barely able to carry me for fear of what I'd find. Then I was there, and my eyes widened... and the scream that left my throat echoed through the barn and out into the street.

A lake of blood covered the floor and Tom's body swayed methodically - his lifeless arms dangling just above the giant pool of blood. Outside I could hear Granger's twisted laughter. Hatred exploded inside me, and I vowed to send him to hell. So, turning, I stepped in the direction of the door leading outside and slipped on Tom Wade's blood and fell.

The floor seemed miles away. Downward I tumbled... with a speed that sent a tingling through my body. Down I dropped, as if having fallen from the top of a Mountain... the floor grew closer, and I could feel myself spinning like the frantic blade of a windmill in a storm. There was no stopping, nor could I scream for the force, and I knew as soon as I struck the floor, my body would shatter like a China Vase.

Then I awoke and bolted straight up in bed. Tom was there and I realized that he'd been shaking my shoulder trying to wake me. He looked worried and I knew he was concerned. With sweat covering my face I looked first him than around the room. He had lit the lantern on the dresser and the place was filled with shadowy light.

"That must have been some dream." He told me sympathetically.

"No." I said, "Nightmare!"

"Are you all right now?"

Nodding, I put my feet over the side of the bed. As I moved, I told him. "It must have been the steak I had for dinner."

Tom squeezed my shoulder, "If that's the case, from now on you order fried chicken only."

My hair was soaking wet, and my body was saturated with perspiration. After drying off with a towel I built a smoke and lit it with shaking hands. I inhaled deeply and it helped calm me down. But my hand continued to tremble slightly, and Tom noticed it.

"Hey, are you sure you are all right?"

Looking at him I forced a smile. "Yeah!."

"What in the world were you dreaming about?"

I blew smoke toward ceiling and told him.

"Granger." That was all I told him. There was no need to say anything else. After all it was just a dream, it meant nothing... nothing at all. I crushed out my cigarette then blew out the lantern.

 Back in bed I pillowed my hands behind my head. In the darkness I laid awake for a long time. I hadn't dreamed like that since childhood. More than ever I wanted for all of this to end. I wondered if the dream could possibly mean something... perhaps an omen or warning.

No." I said to myself, such thinking was silly, but silly or not, it bothered me and for quite some time it kept me awake.

The last thing I remember before drifting off, was asking the good Lord to keep that dream from happening again, but that if he couldn't, then at least let my gun have been in my holster next time.

By 10 the next morning, we were sitting in the fork on the north road. Pausing momentarily, we checked our pistols then continued.

The clerk at the hotel had not lied. The ranch house was BIG. It could easily compare to some of the huge mansions I'd once seen on a trip to Los Angeles. Straight and noble, it reached into the sky. I wondered why anyone would need or want such a big home...other than feeding one's ego, and somehow, I knew that was Booker's reason.

Tom and I were not sure what would happen, or whether Granger would even be at the ranch. If he was we would be ready.

CHAPTER SIXTEEN

At a distance the house appeared big, but once in the yard it became enormous. Three giant pillars stood powerful across the front porch, supporting a beautiful lattace balcony. Even rows of windows trimmed with black shutters gave perfect contrast to a bright white painted exterior that glistened in the warm sun. Encompassing the house was a black iron fence, glossy too in its own right. Between the fence and the house grew a beautiful yard. Multicolored flowers stood proud beneath the warm sun that nourished them, and between the flower beds, green grass that I'm sure Gertrude coveted, grew with a touch of professional husbandry.

Stopping at the gate of the black fence, we dismounted. A small boy of 10 or so came running up and insisted he take our horses for water and brushing. As he pulled them away, I have sworn Gertrude looked back and smiled.

Entering through the gate we made our way up a walkway to the porch. A colored gentlemen dressed in a long tailed, white dinner jacket stepped out to greet us. He was an older fellow with a salt and pepper mustache and head of hair to match. The man had a friendly mannerism and I liked him right away.

"Good morning to ya sir. Do ya wish to speak with Mr. Booker?"

"Yes, we do, thanks." I told him.

"Well, I am sorry sir. But the master is away. Would you all like to speak with Ms. Booker?"

Tom and I looked at one another undecided. Finally, I told him, yes.

"If you all would follow me." He continued, "I'll be more than happy to fetch her for you."

He turned then and we followed him into the house. While stepping into the door I asked him his name and he glanced over his shoulder. "Ruben, sir. They call me Ruben."

Once inside, he excused himself to go for the woman the hotel clerk had made a big deal over, and as he walked away, I yelled after him. "Thank you, Ruben."

Tom and I waited just inside the door. We stood in a large room with beautifully papered walls, covered tastefully with selected paintings. The floor was a polished hardwood and at the far end of the room a carpeted stairway twisted its way up to the higher levels of the house. There was also a hallway leading off somewhere unknown and a giant fireplace in the north corner. To the right of us there was an adjacent room, but the door was closed so we couldn't tell what it was. The place was beautiful.

When Rubin returned, he led us down the hallway to a study that had been done in the finest of leather. Everything was light brown, almost the color red. A giant picture window gave the view of a large fruit orchard that had not been cultivated overnight. Ceiling to floor shelving held hundreds of books and on one wall a massive map of the United States hung framed in glass.

Rubin told us to make ourselves comfortable, that Ms. Booker would be along momentarily. When he left Tom and I sat side by side in twin chairs facing the desk. They were positioned such that our backs were to the doorway, so we turned them slightly.

Five minutes past before Ms. Booker made her entrance. When she came in, we stood. She was tall, probably just a couple inches shorter then my six feet. Her hair was long, black and shined in the sunlight as she moved behind the desk. The dress she wore was made of soft taffeta and tailored well to a slim body.

Once in position, she stood poised, staring at us with big round eyes as blue as the sky over Colorado. Her lips were pursed slightly as she contemplated what she would say. The sight of her sent a fragment of desire through my body.

Then she spoke and I noticed the witness of her teeth, for a split second my mind flashed to the bright white gloss of the paint on the house. I couldn't help thinking how well she seemed to fit here. In a world of class, wealth and education. Her skin was magnificently tanned, and my only thought was of how breathtakingly beautiful she was... and her voice flowed like the soft gentleness of a mountain stream.

She motioned with her hand.

"Please gentlemen, sit down."

She sat as well and began. "Ruben tells me you want to speak to my brother. As I'm sure he has already informed you, Charles is out-of-town on business. However, if there is any way I might be of service to you, please feel free to ask."

I decided not to pull any punches. Tom and I had nothing to lose anyway, and if nothing else this just might get things rolling.

"Yes, Ms. Booker." I told her, "I would like it very nice if you could be of service."

Her eyes squinted for a second and I flushed, realizing I should have worded it differently, but then I saw a ghost of a smile.

The thought of how pleasant she was being came to mind, but I knew it would change the minute we stated our business. Speaking bluntly, I told her.

"We're actually looking for Granger."

The corners of her mouth curled slightly and a small trace of dimples showed on her cheeks. Moving her hands together, she interlaced her fingers and asked.

"Why?"

I was direct. "Because in Colorado, he is wanted for the attempted murder of a United States Marshall.... and because he's a rapist, a thief and a cold blood killer. He murdered a woman and her two children than burned them up in their own house. The man also" I added, "cut the throat of a small-town Sheriff just to leave us a trail to follow. On top of all that the life of a good man depends on his admitting to his crimes."

Allison Booker looked down at the desk top a moment, then back at us.

"I see." She said, "Please correct me if I'm wrong." She was looking directly at me. "You are United States Marshall Steinberge, the one he nearly killed, first by shooting you in the head, then by nearly beating you to death. Am I correct?"

I was not sure how to take what I was hearing. She continued while turning her eyes on Tom. "And your Tom Wade, it was your family he and the others murdered."

Our mouths were wide-open in disbelief, and it was a good thing no flies were around.

Allison Booker's face went sober. "Yes gentlemen, I know all about why you're here. You two have been the main topic of conversation for several days. Not that I'm included in that talk, on the contrary, it's just that I have a, let's say, a more than average curiosity for what goes on in this house."

She paused and looked down at her hands then raised her eyes again to me.

"Am I safe in saying that you loathe Mr. Granger?"

"Hate, Ms. Booker, Hate. And the word has a true ring to it."

Her eyes develop a seriousness. "Yes." She said nodding her head, "that does better suit him. He is easy to hate."

I figured why not get bolder.

"And what about Mr. Booker?" I asked her.

"Oh yes," she began, "my dear Brother Charles. Because he's my brother I love him you understand, but inside he is worse than David,"

"David?" I asked questioningly.

"David Granger, the man you're seeking, obviously you did not know his first name. I'm sorry."

Ruben came into the room and Allison had him bring over three glasses and a bottle of Sheery. As we sat and talked, we sipped the wine slowly and I learned that Allison Booker was as beautiful inside and she was out.

Until age seven she and Charles had lived with her parents in California, at which time they moved here to Tucson. Her father had been a Lawyer but had grown discontented with all of the under-handedness creeping into the legal system. That was why he moved here, to build the cattle empire she, Charles and David Granger stood to inherit. Her father was dead now but her mother, alive and well, had moved back to California leaving all in the hands of the children.

She pointed out Brother Charles had self-appointed himself supreme ruler, much to the disliking of younger brother David, but unfortunately for him, he was only a half-brother and lacked the influence and savvy to oppose.

Granger had been the result of a discrete but brief affair by the mother. Up until the time he had turned bad, it had made no difference to Allison. She had accepted him as much as she had Charles, however, to Charles himself, he had always been little more than a bastard.

Both brothers had bullied their way through life, taking what they wanted and buying that which they couldn't. As for Allison, she was little more than an inconvenience to them both, especially Charles. To him she was but a token he kept around for the appeasement of the mother.

Allison spoke of countless efforts to try and reach her brothers to convince them to change, but they would not listen. There was no going to her mother to explain… she would not believe, and even if she did, Allison said, it was for too late. It was only a matter of time she told us before their power infested minds came up against the wrong people. Now, those people sat in front of her.

As the conversation ended, I asked when Charles would be back.

"I think perhaps in two or three days." she told us.

"And what about Granger? Any idea where he is?"

Allison shook her head. "I'm not sure. Last I heard he was going to Albuquerque on an errand for Charles. With him I never know. He is always coming and going."

As far as I was concerned, all was done here that could be done – except for getting to know Allison better. The wine had warmed me and I wanted to stay and talk with her, but now was not the time.

When we stood to say good-by, Allison shook our hands. To Tom she expressed her sympathy, and when she gave it, I saw a sincerity in her eyes. Tom was moved and I knew he felt the honesty too.

When she took my hand, I thought I felt an extra squeeze, but put it out of my mind. Our eyes locked, we gazed for a moment not saying anything. Strange as it seemed, it was hard to say good-by. Her hand was soft and warm, and I didn't want to let go, and I sensed she felt the same. I had never experienced such a feeling before. In her eyes I saw insecurity, perhaps fear. I wanted to reach out and pull her close, to hold her, to reassure her this would all work out and… then the big picture window behind her exploded, and glass shattered into the room. The bullet zinged past our heads, slamming into the framework around the door.

Impulsively my gun came into my hand, and I grabbed Allison as I dove for the floor. Tom followed suit, then worked his way to the wall beside the window and peered out. No one was in sight. Leaving Allison safely on the floor, I joined him in the search. Minutes passed but we saw no movement. Whoever it had been was now gone. Rubin had just started into the room when the shot was fired. It was only by luck he wasn't struck.

Feeling it was now safe, we rose to our feet, careful of the scattered glass fragments. At least no one was hurt and for that we were all thankful.

CHAPTER SEVENTEEN

Upon our return to town, we kept our eyes open and senses alert. Whoever had fired that shot back at the house could be waiting for us anywhere.

The sky above was growing dark – not just from the approach of evening, but because of dark clouds that threatened to bring rain.

A storm was near, and it would hit sometime during early night fall and by the looks, it would be a bad one.

At the hotel we ordered sandwiches and coffee to be brought up to our room.

Stretched out on the bed Tom and I talked, trying to analyze to date our situation.

The bullet that torn through Allison's window could have been meant for any one of us – Allison included. Who had fired it we'd probably never know. It could have been Granger, but like Charles, he was supposed to be out of town. It had only been one bullet and there very well could have been time for one, maybe two more, before we were all out of sight. That meant one of two things… either the shot was fired an intended miss, designed to only scare us, or, whoever fired at us was inexperienced. Granger could have easily left orders for us to be killed while he was gone, although I doubted it. He wanted to do it himself.

Perhaps the shot was meant to discourage Allison from talking too much, a warning to scare her into silence. If so, what did she know that they did not want her to tell us? The lady was smart, and I doubted that very little went on in the house that she did not know about. While we were there, she had told us much, although most of it had been of little significance.

There had been one truly encouraging thing though, the fact she had heard Granger confess to the murders of Tom's family. Her testimony could make a difference to a jury if she agreed to testify.

By six the sky was black and distant thunder could be heard rumbling every few minutes. There was no rain as yet, but it was just a matter of time.

I lit the lantern, and it filled the hotel room with a soft, easy light. We still wondered about the business deal between Granger and Booker. It could be anything? But whatever it was, we were willing to bet our saddles it was on the shady side.

There was a knock on the door then. After looking at one another, we rose from the bed and took our pistols in hand. We were expecting the food we'd ordered, but caution was now the way we needed to live.

Tom went to answer the door while I waited by the dresser, gun in hand. When he opened it the desk clerk smiled.

"Evening gents," He said cheerfully, He held up a tray covered with a small linen sheet saying, "Delivery of food you ordered."

Holding the smile, the clerk peaked around Tom's shoulder at me. Letting me know Chipper made it himself – personally. "Especially for you Mr. Steinberge."

He handed it to Tom and left.

"Gee, Arch," Tom said with a grin, "Who do you think Chipper could be?"

Sober faced I told Tom Wade to shut up and holstered my gun.

The sandwiches were tasty, but the coffee really hit the spot. By the time we were finished, the thunder had drawn close, and lightening was streaking across the sky. Still no rain, but now it could be any minute.

Around eight o'clock there came a second knock on the door. This time we were expecting no one. As before, we grabbed our guns, and I went to the dresser while Tom answered.

When he opened it, a small boy stood looking up at him. When the youngster spoke, there was nervousness in his voice.

"Is there a Mr. Steinbirth here?"

"You mean Mr. Steinberge?"

The boy raised his eyebrows, not really sure.

"Yes sir, I think so?"

Stepping to the door so he could see me I peered down at him. He recognized me immediately. It was the little kid who had taken our horses for water and brushing at the Booker Ranch.

Smiling to help put him at ease I stuck out my hand and offered him my shake. He took it and almost instantly we saw the tenseness go away. Then Tom shook his hand and that made the kid grin.

"Now young man," I said, "I'm Mr. Steinberge, what can I do for you?"

He was a cute lad. His eyes were big and alive and full of mischief. Straight, sandy colored hair fell across his forehead, almost in his eyes and like Allison, he had the cutest little dimples on his cheeks. The neat clothes he wore enhanced his polite mannerism and both Tom and I were impressed.

"Sir," he started in, "Ms. Booker would like to see you at the ranch house. She said to tell you it was important."

"Do you know what about?" I asked.

He shrugged his shoulders.

"No sir, she didn't say. But she did want me to say that you come alone."

I looked at Tom and his eyes met mine. Worry lines showed around his eyes.

"I don't like it Arch. It doesn't settle right."

"I know." I said, "But what choice do we have? It may be our one chance to get to Granger."

Tom shook his head. "It may be a trap taking you right to Granger."

I realized it was a risk. But risks were what my job was all bout — and sometimes death too. I would just have to look before I leaped.

I touched Tom's shoulder.

"Don't worry, pal, I'll be careful."

Then I looked down at the boy.

"Well, my little friend, looks like we can ride back together."

The boy shook his head.

"No sir. Ms. Booker gave me orders to stay in town because of the storm."

"Stay in town where?" I asked him.

He made a terrible face. "With my Aunt Sara."

Hiding my grin, I asked. "Do you by any chance not like Aunt Sara?"

He stuck his hands in his pockets and kicked at the floor with his boot toe.

"She's OK I reckon. It's just that she treats me like a baby all the time. She calls me Georgie."

His face turned red. Keeping my face sober, I asked.

"Well, what do you like to be called. Tell us and that's what we will call you."

He looked up at the both of us and smiled. The dimples really coming alive.

"The guys at school call my Buddy. It's my nickname."

Tom leaned against the door jam and folded his arms. Smiling down at him he said. "Tell you what Buddy, while Mr. Steinberge is away we'll stay right here for a while and play some cards. Around ten, which should be about bedtime, I'll walk you to Aunt Sara's house. That way she'll put you right to bed and only get to call you Georgie once… when she kisses you good night. Does that sound pretty good?"

The boy lit up like a candle in a dark root cellar.'

"Yes sir, it sounds mighty fine."

When I left, there was apprehension in Tom's eyes and he warned to be careful.   Careful was not the half of it. Sneaky, distrusting and gun ready was more like it.

As Gertrude and I left the stable, lightening flashed across the dark sky above our heads. For only a second, I thought I saw the shadow of a man standing near the alley at the hotel. By the time the second flash came there was nothing.

Gertrude and I headed north out of town and as I rode, I wondered to myself… what exactly was the reason Allison was calling me out? At the house earlier she had seemed understanding and open. She had shown compassion for Tom… or was it just an act? The woman was beautiful, the envy of many a man in Town I was sure, however sometimes beauty was not what it seemed. To me there was nothing to match the splendid, rugged beauty of the Colorado Rockies…and that lady had killed more than her fair share of unsuspecting men. I would just have to be cautious.

Just this side of the fork the rain started. It fell easy at first – small drops barely noticeable. The sky was nearly void of any stars and a deep blackness hid the world from me until lightening flashed. I did my best to utilize the fractions of light to watch the area around me. If someone was following or waiting for me, it would be only by change that I'd see them. In the dark it would be hard to find the house if I were to leave the road. So like it or not, staying on it was what I needed to do.

Then the hard rain began. It fell in mad, hammering sheets. A savage down fall soaked me inside and out in a matter of minutes. The air grew cold fast, and I felt myself begin to shiver. My already heavy coat was now even heavier from the weight of the water.

I remembered from our visit earlier in the day, that the barn was to the right of the house a good hundred feet.

I would stop there first and tie Gertrude just inside, near the door where she's stay dry.

When I spotted the house, I dismounted and led her far around the perimeter until I reached the barn from the side. Then, keeping a close eye on the house, I opened the barn door and pulled her in. After tying her, I slipped back out and cautiously started across the yard.

As I approached, I watched the area around me for movement each time lightening flashed.

The main floor area of the house was well lighted. Upstairs on the second floor only a couple rooms glowed with light, one at the front and one at the east side. The third floor was totally dark.

Making my way to the porch, I crouched low moving from window to window. Allison sat alone in the living room dressed in what looked like her night clothes. Why I wondered, would anyone expecting company be waiting dressed for bed? Moving on the east side I did the same thing, checking each window. Nothing. At the back side, I saw a sign of life once again. Rubin was in the kitchen pouring a cup of coffee. Should I go in quietly through the back door and approach him? No, I thought, too risky.

Moving on, I went around the corner to the west side and that's where I got a closer look at Allison. She was sitting near the fireplace on a sofa, reading a book. There seemed to be no one else in the house…

but what about the lights in the rooms upstairs? Were they empty with candles burning for no reason, or was someone in them? Other servants perhaps?

Moving once more to the back of the house, I peered in through the window in the door. Rubin was gone. Trying the doorknob, I found it unlocked. So gingerly I eased it open and slipped inside. My gun was in my hand.

The kitchen was large and exited into the same hallway we had walked down earlier in the day. Quietly I made my way over to the entrance. It was dark like a long tunnel, with no light of its own. At the far end where it opened to the parlor in which Allison sat reading, hazy shadows flickered on the walls.

There was no way of knowing where Rubin had gone, perhaps to a room upstairs? Standing quiet, I listened. I could hear the crackle of the burning wood in the fireplace and somewhere down the darkened hallway in one of the rooms, a clock ticked away.   Outside the rain continued to fall, bombarding the house and splashing into the already standing puddles of water.

What I was listening for was the sound of footsteps across the floor above me, but there had been none. Maybe I was way off base acting so suspicious – so distrusting.

It could just be that Allison did have something important to tell me. Nevertheless now was not the time to start trusting anyone. I had trusted Stone and it nearly cost us greatly.

With careful steps, I inched my way down the hallway toward the room in which Allison sat. My clothes were soaking wet and irritated me. I wished I were back at the hotel room where I could change into something dry, but what did it matter I thought, I still had the long ride back and it too would be in the rain.

At the end of the hallway, I pressed myself against the wall and peered around the corner toward Allison. Her back was to me and except for her, the room was empty. I could feel the heat from the fire on my face.

For several minutes I waited there in the shadows listening. Still, I had heard no sounds out of the ordinary. I knew I couldn't just stand there all night, so leaving the security of the darkness I rounded the corner and inched my way up behind her. The book she was reading must have been interesting for she never turned around until I broke the silence. .

"A good book?"

Startled, she jumped and turned half around to look up at me. Almost immediately she smiled. A beautiful smile.

"Oh Arch, I'm so glad to see you. May I call you Arch?"

She climbed to her feet and stood facing me.

"Yes." I said, "As long as you don't call me Archibald. My mother use to call me that every time I'd do something bad. Which seemed almost all the time growing up."

Her smile was radiant. "Does she still have to call you Archibald?"

"No. She's dead."

Allison's smile disappeared. "Oh, I'm sorry."

Holstering the colt, I said.

"I'm just kidding. My mother is still alive and happy living in Denver. But yes, she does continue to call me Archibald… occasionally now."

Allison smiled again. "I'm beginning to understand why."

Moving around the sofa, I went to the fireplace and stood near its warmth, turning so I could face Allison and the two entrances and stairway at the back of the room.

When she got a good look at me, she made a sympathetic face and said,

"My goodness, look at you. You're soaking wet. Why you'll catch a death of cold."

Walking to the opposite side of the fireplace, she grabbed a hanging cord and pulled it twice.

Watching her I said. "Let me guess. When you pull the line, which runs upstairs through the floor into Rubin's room it rings a little bell?"

"My aren't we observant." She said coyly.

Allison was right, I was observant. But I just wanted to stay alive. The little bell could have been calling someone other than Rubin.

As we continued to talk, I kept my back to the fire and eyes on the entrances into the room. Occasionally I glanced toward the window, but it was more habit than help. Outside blackness prevailed and except during flashes there was no chance of seeing anyone.

Then carrying a candle, Rubin descended the stairway. As soon as he spotted me, he spoke cheerfully.

"Evening Master Steinberge."

I nodded. "Good to see you again Rubin. But it's Mr."

Allison looked at him saying. "Rubin, Mr. Steinberge is soaked to the bone, please go to Mr. Booker's room and bring down a change of clothes for him."

She looked me up and down with her eyes then added. "I believe they are both about the same size – although I'm sure Mr. Steinberge will look a lot more manly in them."

I started to protest but it was a waste of time.

Allison gently placed her soft hand over my mouth and puckered her lips whispering, shhhh!" What could I say?

As soon as Rubin was gone, she began unbuttoning my coat. When it was off, her hands went to my shirt. When she had undone the last button and it lay open, I grabbed her wrists and pulled her against me, starring into her eyes. She grinned and I could feel a stirring inside of me. Her breasts were soft and lay partially flattened against my wet chest. The silken night clothes she wore grew wet as I held her. Our eyes were locked, and we stood staring in silence. Her mouth parted and the look in her eyes invited me.

Then Rubin came into the room, and I released her. As she stepped back, the wetness of her silk top was obvious and for a second, just before she turned so Rubin could not see, I glimpsed her quickened breath and feminine reaction, a man loves to see.

When Rubin handed me the pile of clothes, I thought I saw a faint glimmer of a smile. He said to Allison, "If that will be all Ms. Booker, I will retire to my room for the night and remain there, unless called?"

Looking over at him Allison flashed a second long smile and replied, "Yes, thank you Rubin."

Then he was gone, and we were alone.

At first the moment was awkward. Then she looked at me and grinned.

"You could at least take your hat off in the presence of a lady."

Realizing I was still wearing it I reached up and pulled it off my head. A small run of water fell from it and splattered on the floor at my feet.

"Sorry." I apologized.

She laughed. A throaty, heartfelt laugh. I followed suit.

Looking down at the floor I saw the large puddle of water in which I stood.

Feeling kind of silly, I looked at her, "I guess it really didn't matter, did it?"

"Correct." she said, "It could be a river and it wouldn't matter. But what does matter, is that you get out of those wet clothes. If you like, although I prefer not, I will turn my back."

Her eyes were alive with blue highlighted by the firelight. Soft shadows covered her face and body. Her long hair had been gathered up and pinned neatly on the top of her head. The heat from the fire was already drying her silky clothing and her skin looked sensuously soft. I had liked her touch, it was exciting… intoxicating.

"Well." She said waiting.

"Well, what?"

She laughed again. "Well, what shall it be… watch or turn?"

"You're leaving it up to me?" I asked.

"Yes." She said with a sultry smile.

"Then I'd like you to help. Like before, earlier, before Rubin came in." Her smile widened.

"Marshal Steinberge, is this one of those times when I should be calling you Archibald?"

"That depends," I said.

"Oh, on what?"

"On whether I'm good or bad."

"That answer doesn't even require thought."

She pulled the pin from her hair and shook her head; it fell to her shoulders. "The question of good or bad, doesn't even require thought. I am a woman and tonight, I know, for certain you will be an Archibald. Because tonight, while you are being bad, you will be very, very good."

CHAPTER EIGHTEEN

We made love there by the fire light on a soft oval rug. Outside, thunder crashed, and lightening streaked the sky. The falling rain hammered against the window and together our bodies blended… the perfect match of giving and taking. Pleasure was ours and it was special, and until the very first speck of morning light, we remained in one another arms. When it came time to dress and return to the different worlds in which we lived, there was a shared disappointment.

We were dressed and sitting on the sofa when Rubin descended the stairs. Allison sent him to the kitchen to prepare breakfast while she led me back into the study where we had shared the wine at our first meeting.

I sat in the same chair while she, like before, went around behind the desk. After sitting, she pulled open a drawer and took out a small pile of papers and a green ledger. Leaning across the desk she handed them to me than sat back and spoke.

"I think you will find these of particular interest."

Having no idea of what was going on; I gave her a puzzled look then sat back myself. I crossed my legs and began rummaging through the pile.

The ledger was filled with names, most of whom I didn't recognize – but some I did. Beside each name over in the right-hand column were dollar amounts. Obviously, something was being sold or purchased. Just in front of each dollar figure was a number and this number always varied, ranging from eight to as high as on hundred and twenty-three. Some of the names had a check mark in front of them and others did not. Perhaps it had something to do with payment. But payment for what I wondered.

Leaving the ledger, I concentrated on the pile of papers. The first was an envelope. Reaching in I pulled out a neatly folded letter and opened it. It was a short but interesting note, addressed to Charles Booker.

Charles,

Received the shipment on time. Recipients were pleased. Vic wants more. Payment is in fine shape. See you on the 3rd for pick-up.

Mat

The letter was dated the fifteenth of last month. Was that the pick-up day mentioned for this coming month? If so, that is probably where Charles was this very moment.

I searched the envelope for a return address but there was none. There were four more letters from the same man saying about the same thing and none of those had a return address either, why?

Within the pile I also found a sheet of paper with a bunch of figuring on it. It was more scribbling than anything else. No sense could be made of it.

Opening the ledger once more, I scanned the names. There were twenty-two all together. Of them, I recognized five. Two were businessmen from Colorado - one from Denver and the other from Colorado Springs. And there was a third man from Colorado as well, the Sheriff from Durango. The fourth name was also a long-time deputy with the Sheriff's Office in Cheyenne, Wyoming. As for the fifth name – it was one I knew very well… myself. Allison saw it on my face.

"See," she said smiling, "I told you would find it interesting."

Rubin came in and announced breakfast, I handed the stuff back to Allison and warned her.

"Put them back exactly the way you found them. Whatever you do, never let Charles or Granger know you saw them, and especially that you showed them to me."

As she put them back, I looked out into the orchard beyond the broken window. Rubin had boarded most of it up, but there remained some glass and through it I watched as the sun began to raise high above the trees.

I rose from the chair and Allison came around to join me. Taking her in my arms we kissed – and I could feel a special warmth. In such a short time Allison and I had grown close. Kiss over, she wrapped her arms around my neck and laid her head on my shoulder. I pulled her close, not believing I had been blessed with such a beautiful and loving woman. Then she turned her head and whispered in my ear. "Arch, am I feeling you turn into an Archibald again?"

A little past eight, I closed the door behind me and walked to the barn. The air was cool, but the feel of a beautiful day was everywhere. I hated to leave, but there was little choice.

Inside the barn door I stopped cold. Gertrude was not where I had left her. My saddle and blanket were hanging over a stall gate and she had been boarded for the night. A nice gesture, but by who? Rubin maybe, perhaps he had come down and put her up for the night as soon as he realized I was going to spend the evening.

Then I heard a faint stirring in a stall to my right. It was the sound of rustling hay. To be safe I eased the .44 out of its holster. That was when Tom stepped out, rubbing sleep from his eye and brushing hay from his clothes.

"Thomas Washington Wade, What the heck are you doing here?"

Stopping the rubbing and brushing he made a face.

"Is that anyway to greet a friend. If you must know, I've been baby-sitting."

"BABY SITTING?"

"Yeah."

"For whom?"

"For you."

"What do you mean, for me?"

Sticking his hat on top of his head, he continued.

"Well, when you didn't come back to the hotel by two, I got worried. So, I rode out to check on things. To see if you need my help. When I got here it was obvious you had things under control. But it was too late to ride back and I just decided to wait here. So, here I am."

I holstered my gun.

"Just like that, here you are."

"Yeah, just like that here I am."

Almost afraid to ask, I said. "And just what did you see when you arrived?"

Tom's grin was long, and it turned me red. Then he said.

"To be honest, nothing. You were both sleeping near the fire."

I felt a sense of relief wash over me, but I told him.

"You know, I appreciate your concern partner, but don't you think I'm big enough to take care of myself? I stopped needing a babysitter long ago."

Tom threw up his hands. "OK, OK. I'm sorry. I should have realized you're a grown-up boy. Now can we please saddle up and get out of here? I need a bath and breakfast."

When I agreed he gave a sigh of relief but added.

"And Arch, you needn't worry?"

I looked at him questioningly, "Needn't worry about what?"

Tom grinned wider. "I won't tell Chipper."

Back in town we stopped off at the bath house and soaked a long time in a tub of hot, soapy water. The air outside the tub was chilly, but the water inside was perfect. As we soaked, we each smoked a cigarette. Both tubs were near a big window and rays from the warm sun filtered in extra heat. It was a good feeling to be clean and to taste the smoke of a good cigarette.

As we sat soaking, I told Tom about the ledger and the names I had found written in it. The same ones I had recognized he knew as well. The picture was still not clear. There was some kind of business deal going on, but what it was we had no idea yet. What was interesting was why my name was in the ledger? Probably for their protection.

It was really a smart move. How could I turn in such a thing for evidence against Granger or Booker, and not be incriminating myself. And I was sure that a duplicate ledger lay hidden somewhere. The Colorado names were on the same page in a row. If I destroyed the page with my name on it, I destroyed all the other names.

So, there it was once again in a tidy little package. Tom Wade the hunted man, could only be cleared by a criminal who I needed to keep alive, but wanted to kill. It was no wonder Granger had beat me half to death after shooting me, then worried not one little iota about rubbing it in. He knew he had me by the tail and there was no way I could bite back. Now, if I wanted to save Tom I had to worry about my own neck. In short, if I tried to take Granger or Booker down – I went with them.

We soaked an hour then returned to the hotel. At noon we went to the 'other' restaurant and had lunch. It wasn't as fancy as the first, but the food was every bit as good. After we had eaten, we talked over coffee.

I asked Tom his opinion on what to do next.

"I really don't know Arch", he began thoughtfully, "It seems we're both in a tight clinch now. These guys are no fools. They certainly know how to play the game, and they play to win."

"Yeah. But there's one thing they've not thought out."

"What's that?"

"While they seem to have things sewn up within the legal realm, in the end, the true winners will be the ones left alive after the bullets stop flying."

Tom took a sip of coffee then set his cup down. It clinked quietly against the saucer. "To be honest Arch, I really don't care much about all this legal garbage they've got going, except of course for the fact you're now caught in the middle of it. All I really want is Granger. I want to stand face to face with him. I don't care if it's with guns, knives, clubs or fists. All I know is he killed my family and he's going to pay. I want him bad."

"I know, partner", I told him, "And I know too that it hurts. Just remember, as long I'm alive you've got a friend at your side. A friend who'll die if he must. But I've got an idea."

Tom waited to hear me out.

It was a sensitive question I was about to ask, and I knew Tom would get his feathers ruffled. "Look", I told him, "What if we let Granger go for now!" He looked at me coldly, as if I'd said something insane. Waiving my hand I added, "Easy now, hear me out. Why don't we return to Denver, be there in a few days and pay a visit to the persons whose names appear on the ledger. If we can find out what's going on we may find a way out of this mess. What do you say?"

He hesitated a long while. The waitress came by and refilled our coffee cups. It was hot and I watched the steam rise. As Tom continued to think I told him. "I really doubt Granger is going anywhere. He and Booker both think they're a couple of fat cats. A visit back may give us the insight we need to clear all this up. I really think it's the right thing to do, Tom."

He took a sip of coffee than looked over at me saying, "OK. We give it four days. Then we're back here and we don't stop until we have Granger."

There was hate in his eyes and I knew he was agreeing only because of our friendship. Taking a sip of coffee, I went silent, lost in thought. I could only hope I was making the right decision and doing the right thing for him… and for me too.

CHAPTER NINETEEN

Leaving Tucson, we rode south to Bisbee insuring we were not being followed. That was where we'd board the train so as not to tip off Granger. We did not want word getting to the men we planned to visit.

At the depot we sat through a two hour wait and it was around 3:00pm when we heard the blow of the whistle. Walking outside we stood on the platform and watched the train's slow approach.

There were three other people waiting, a husband and wife and a young man of seventeen or so, he was holding a small suitcase and I wondered if maybe he was on his way to join the Army.

As it lugged toward us the train began to take shape. When we had first come out it was but a small black speck in the distance. Now it was becoming a recognizable mass of giant iron, belching smoke and laying on the whistle.

Gertrude, along with Tom's horse would ride the cattle car behind us. Where I went, she went. After all, she was my sweetheart…and although I'd never tell her, back in Tucson, for the first time, Gertrude was facing competition.

As the train pulled into the station, I watched a skinny, ribbed dog run along beside barking at the wheels. There was no hearing him for the noise, but I could see his mouth move as he chased it along. The train was small, only one passenger coach with a cattle car behind it and a caboose at the end.

Tom and I chose seats at the rear of the coach where he beat me to the window. There were eleven others aboard – three couples, a family of four and one man dressed in jeans, a black shirt with matching hat and a gun he wore low on his hip. And like us, he sat near the back where he could watch what went on. There had been one other horse in the cattle car, and it was probably his.

The train rocked monotonously along. There was something in its motion that made you want to sleep, and Tom and I both catnapped off and on.

Outside there was not a lot to see, occasional cactus, sagebrush and cedar scrub covering the desert floor. Above, a hot sun boiled down on the car and the open windows helped circulate a little cool air, which we all appreciated.

At a good speed, we pushed along the narrow tracks, pouring smoke into a sky almost as blue as Allison's eyes. I thought about her.

She certainly was something, a cowboy's dream. The night we had spent together I would remember the rest of my life. It was something I'd like to spend the rest of my life doing, but smiling I shook my head.

I couldn't picture Allison Booker as Mrs. Steinberge. She was upper society, bound to marry a doctor or a lawyer or some other such successful man. Her future could not include life with a Federal Marshal, constantly living in a worrisome state, wondering if each day marked the end of my life and the start of hers… as a widow!

Except for the occasional appearance of a small mountain formation, the scenery remained repetitious. Always, the Train rocked, and the floor vibrated beneath our feet.

Allison was not in a good situation. I feared for her safety should Booker suspect what she had shown us. Realizing she was his sister, I figured on that as accounting for something. However, Booker's first and foremost priority was maintaining power, and God help anyone who should get in his way.

We traveled into New Mexico to Las Cruces, and then turned north, moving up toward Albuquerque. The hours passed slowly.

For dinner Tom and I shared beef jerky and warm water. It wasn't particularly filling, but if did keep my stomach from rumbling. At 8:10pm we pulled to a stop at the Albuquerque depot. There were six people waiting to board and I recognized one of them. He was one of the men that had held my arms the day Granger had beaten me.

The coach was dark from the dim lantern light so I guessed he would not spot me. I wanted him to, mind you.

As a matter of fact, it would have been nice to introduce myself. But now was not the time. He probably was going to Denver on an errand for Granger. Watching him might prove more rewarding than returning the beating he had helped give to me… although I felt it did merit the toss of a coin.

He was sitting in a seat near the middle of the coach, and I watched him rock to the rhythm of the train as we pushed on toward the Colorado line.

What was Granger and Booker up to? I thought about the ledger Allison had shown me. It was filled with prominent names – men Booker no doubt owned and had paid off for some type of service. And what of the letters from the man called Matt? He was delivering some type of merchandise, but what, and to whom? The two men we were going to see were both well-to-do. Robert Frankons of Colorado Springs was a businessman who owned stores, saloons and ranches across both Colorado and Wyoming. The second man, Ralph Burroes, was a Banker and rancher in Denver. And like Charles Booker he was a man of influence and power when he wanted to push it. I wondered what it was, if anything, these men had in common? Sure, they were all rich and all had made their fortune through cattle, but this was something bigger than a private social club.

Taking a deep draw from my cigarette I said out loud.

"And horses!"

Tom glanced my way. "What?"

Dropping my butt, I crushed it out then looked at him.

"Booker, Burroes and Frankons are all cattlemen."

"Yeah, so?"

"So, there's also one other thing they have in common. Horses. They deal in cattle and horses."

"What's the point?"

Frowning I told him. "I don't know. It may mean nothing. It's just common ground that's all."

Dropping the subject, I looked past Tom and out the window. Night had engulfed us. Outside, the moon was full, and it cast a bright light over the desert. Stars twinkled in the blackness, and I caught a glimpse of the big dipper. The whistle blew and we started up a steep grade.

Joining Tom, I pulled my hat over my eyes and laid my head against the back of the seat. "Horses," I said under my breath, "Horses, Horses, Horses."

*

We pulled into Colorado Springs around midnight. Allowing Granger's man to get off first we made sure he was out of sight before leaving to retrieve the horses. This would be the end of our train ride. In the morning we would visit Frankons, then ride on to Denver to talk with Burroes.

Hiding in the shadows, we watched to see what Granger's man would do. He left the terminal and walked to the livery where he rented a horse, then rode out into the darkness. That ended one mystery for us, the third Horse was not his.

Tom and I made camp in the rocks just outside of town. After a quick dinner of bacon and hard tack, we rolled out our bed blankets. We had built the fire in the rocks where it could not be seen unless stumbled upon by accident. And to keep from taking any chances, we took three-hour watches.

The hotel would have been nice, but now that we were back in our own neck of the woods, Tom would have to be extra careful, there were just too many who knew him. And even with the telegram I carried, there were still men to whom it would mean nothing. Besides, things hadn't changed – if we did run into trouble, we preferred it to be in the daylight.

It was cold and we slept in our coats. Throughout the night, coyotes howled into the darkness and the fire flames danced to a strong chilly wind. While on guard, I watched Tom toss and turn restlessly beneath his blanket. The night air encouraged me to pull my own blanket tight around me. There was no doubt, I admitted to myself, I was growing too old for this kind of long-time-away kind of work anymore.

We broke camp at the first show of light. The morning air numbed our fingers, and we could see our breath.

In town we stopped off at the only restaurant opened and ordered bacon and eggs. While waiting for it to arrive, we sipped coffee and talked.

Frankon had an office here in town and would be in about the time we finished eating. Who knew what we might find out? Probably he'd tell us nothing by playing dumb. What I really wished was to go through his desk with him not around. It we were to get anything out of him at all, it would have to be scared out, which should not be a big problem. Robert Frankon was a fat, cowardly man who, without his money, would probably live his life out of a bottle. He certainly liked his whiskey and many of the other vices in life as well.

When breakfast arrived, the bacon was just the way I like it, crispy, the eggs sunny side up and the waitress never once let our cups go dry. By the time we were finished, the sun was well up into the sky and its golden light covered a good part of the town. The streets were coming alive with people and many of the businesses were opening their doors. Merchants swept their walkways, men and women chatted and down the street we could hear the clang of the blacksmith's hammer.

Not wanting to spend a lot of time in the streets, we left the restaurant and walked directly to Frankon's office.

His secretary was a young, attractive woman in a calico dress of light blue. Her eyes were big and pretty and sparkled when she talked. She informed us that Mr. Frankons was not in yet. That it was unusual for him to be late, but we were welcomed to wait. So, wait we did.

The pretty secretary began building a fire in the office stove and Tom helped her with the wood.

Outside, the streets were growing busier. There was a lot of horse and buggy activity now and I wondered where all the people were coming from.

We waited nearly forty minutes. When Frankons didn't show, we got directions to his house and left. His place was nearly two miles out of town and was no problem finding.

When we knocked on the door no one answered. I tried the handle. It was not locked so after looking over my shoulder we slipped inside the house. The place was quiet and cold. We stood in a nicely decorated living room with a huge beautifully shined Mahogany Fireplace. In one corner of the room, a small round table lay tipped on its side with two broken wine glasses and a decanter shattered over the floor. It appeared that there had been some type of struggle. The ashes in the fireplace were cold and had been out probably six or seven hours. I didn't like it.

Tom investigated the kitchen and found nothing out of the ordinary. Why was the house empty? Shouldn't there be a wife or at least a servant or two about?

With caution we searched the rest of the house. In a bedroom at the east end, we found the body of a young woman, perhaps the maid, lying on the floor near the bed. Her head had been bashed – probably by the blunt end of a pistol butt. Her body was cold, and we guessed she died about the same time the fire did.

Upstairs we found Frankons. He was lying in his own bed, propped up on pillows, staring blankly at the doorway through which we stepped. There were two bullet holes, side by side in his forehead, and behind him the pillows lay covered with his brains. Someone obviously did not wish for him to talk with us.

Suddenly I thought of Allison and swore under my breath.

CHAPTER TWENTY

With Frankons dead that left Burroes, and it was my guess Granger's assassin was on his way there right now.

We had one chance to beat him to his next victim – travel by train. In addition, I'd send a telegram to my office and have a guard put on him just to make sure.

The train to Denver was not do in until 11:30 am, so we took a visit to Frankons Office one more time. It appeared I'd get my wish after all. The secretary turned pale and had to sit when we told her the bad news. Once recovered though, I explained we were lawmen and she let us into Frankons office without question.

We found nothing. There were three drawers in his desk, but only one had been locked. And, had, was the stressed word, someone prior to our visit, had forced it open and papers lay strewn over the floor. Damn, I thought. It seemed they were always one step ahead. When we had left Tucson, we were sure no one was the wiser. Perhaps it was just coincidence, but I doubted it.

Immediately upon sending the telegram to my office, we grabbed a quick bite then caught the train. During the trip Tom struck up a conversation with the conductor. He was an old busy body who liked to talk. According to him the Indian situation was growing worse. There had been several more killings of settlers and it was spreading.

According to the Army the Sioux were returning from Canada and secretly massing in great numbers. It was believed their intention was to reunite and take back their lands. There were also rumors of the great Geronimo, chief of the Chiricahuas Apache, banding his people.

The names of other great chiefs and warriors came up too, like Nachez, Nana and the son of Cochise. The names were many and the situation, if truthful, was sad. For many people, Indian and white alike, would die. As in the past the Indian could not hope to win but would fight bravely trying.

Having fought in the past Indian Campaigns I knew only too well the devastation a new uprising would bring. Someone was stirring them up. Someone with influence and power, and someone who stood to gain from such a war. This person might be a rancher selling beef to the Army for food, and horses for the Calvary to ride. And if this individual was doing all of that, he would do whatever else he could to keep the war effort going… like selling guns to the Indians on the side.

It was all beginning to make sense now. The ledger, the letters signed by the man named matt, the murder of Frankons and the merging of all the appropriate people. Cattlemen, Ranchers and Bankers…were all the ingredients needed for a successful Indian War. And with a steady supply of guns to the Indians, there would be a long run of profit.

Suddenly I hated Booker as much as Granger. So many innocent people would die while he coldly looked the other way to count his money.

He needed to be stopped. The Indian uprising needed to be stopped. But how? If I could get my hands on that ledger again and turn it over as evidence, it just might put him behind bars. In addition, a confession from Allison would almost make it a sure thing.

At this very moment I wished I had not decided to come to Denver. In my heart and way down deep in my gut I had a terrible feeling. Suddenly I wanted to be at Allison's side. Concern for her lay like a heavy weight over me. It was silly, unjustified. Yet inside the uneasiness made me weak.

She was valuable as a witness. Allison's lone confession could literally make or break a case against her brother. The bottom line was that her words could mean the difference between life and death for hundreds of people throughout the western lands. If Charles Booker was not stopped soon, senseless killing would sweep the west like a terrible plague.

As the train rolled north toward Denver, Tom and I discussed our case. Without the ledger there was no way we could have anyone arrested. The fact that my name appeared in it was now of little concern... to many lives were at stake. While in Denver I would visit the Governor's Office and explain what was going on, what happened after that would be up to him.

How much help Burroes would be was anyone's guess. If he was told about Frankons it might make a difference, but only time would tell.

The train rolled into Denver at precisely 1:14pm, a light snow was falling, but the sky was clear. As we stepped from the train, Tom stopped and took a long look around. For him it was undoubtedly a good feeling to be home... even if he was at risk.

After unloading the horses, we rode straight to my office at the jail. Luck was with us. Billy Patterson was on duty. He was young and full of sass, but he was one fine Lawman. When he saw us come in, he looked surprised then smiled. Coming over to greet us he stuck out his hand and welcomed me back. Then turning to Tom, he said, "You old horses rear, I damn near didn't recognize ya." He hugged him then and welcomed him home.

Billy told us they had been guarding Burroes since receiving my telegram, and that there had been rumors that Tom was with me and that he was doing fine. They had also heard about my message from the governor and had all sent their well-wishes with it. While at the office,

I pinned another badge on my shirt. It felt good… but I still intended to take the other one back.

After a good cup of coffee and enjoyable conversation with Billy, Tom and I left.   When we walked into the bank several people recognized us and said hello and as we passed by, we could hear them whisper.

At the door of Burroes's office sitting in a chair was Phil Shank, the deputy assigned to guard him. When he saw us, he stood and smiled, then shook our hands and welcomed us back. I told him to sit back down and relax.

When we walked to Burroes he looked right at me and slowly rose from his chair. His face was white, and I didn't know if it was from anger or fear. Then he looked at Tom and after a moment of staring pointed a finger.

"What is he doing here?" When he looked down and saw the gun Tom was wearing, he said. "And what in the hell is he doing wearing a gun? The man's a criminal."

I smiled at him then took out my makings and rolled a cigarette. When it was lit, I said.

"The man's in my custody. It seems that lately I can trust criminals more than upstanding citizens."

Burroes looked at me and knew exactly what I meant. But he didn't say anything, instead, he sat back down and looked up at me. After pulling a cigar from a box and lighting it he said harshly. "So, tell me Steinberge, just what in the hell do you want? And what's the big idea of having me followed and watched by your…" he glanced at Tom then back to me, "other worthless deputies?"

I wanted to pull him across the desk but restrained myself. Instead, I sat in a chair across from him and grinned. "Have you heard about your friend Frankons?"

"No. What about him?"

I watched his face as I talked. "It seems someone decided he shouldn't live anymore and killed him. Shot him twice in the head. His brains were all over the pillow in his bedroom. Such a terrible sight it was, wasn't it Tom?"

Tom cut in. "Yeah. And by the way Mr. Burroes, do you know a fellow by the name of Charles Booker?"

His face developed worry lines, but he played dumb. "No, should I?"

"That depends." Tom told him.

"On what?" Burroes asked.

"On how much you value your life."

Burroes played the part well but there was controlled fear in his voice. "Wade," he said trying to hide the nervousness, "I have no idea what in the hell you are talking about."

Tom smiled for him. "Well, if you don't know him, then I guess you don't have to worry about trusting him. The guy is in a lot of trouble and to protect himself he's having people murdered."

Burroes hands were shaking slightly, and he tried to hide it. But he wasn't doing too well.

I stood up. The conversation had gone the way we expected. Hopefully, it put a scare into him, and he would stop participating any farther. As we left his office, I looked over my shoulder and spoke.

"Better hire a bodyguard, as of now, my worthless deputies will protect you no longer." Phil stood from his chair, looked puzzled at Burroes and followed us out.

Outside the snow was still falling and the temperature was growing colder. The clear sky was turning gray and there was little blue left. By dark a storm would hit, and rain would fall. Mixed with the snow it would cover everything with thick ice.

Tomorrow we would catch the train back to Tucson, back to the only witness in this whole mess… back to Allison Booker.

The governor was still away, but I had a good conversation with Lt. Governor Tabor. We had been friends for some time, and I fully trusted him, however, while I talked with him, Tom waited outside of town. I explained the whole situation, including Booker, Granger, the ledger with my name in it, Allison and what I thought up to date. It was suggested we go back to Tucson and gather what evidence we could then return to Denver.

If Allison would be willing to testify, I was to give her protection and bring her back as well, at the expense of the city of Denver. I told the Lt. Governor I fully understood and would do whatever was necessary to keep her safe… and satisfied.

As for Tom's predicament there was no immediate solution. Again, what Allison Booker would be willing to say to a jury could make all the difference. With each passing moment it seemed she was becoming more and more valuable.

When I left the Lt. Governor's office I had a signed letter from him, granting Tom Wade temporary amnesty for the crimes he had committed. As for reinstating him as a deputy, we weren't sure legally, but to quote the Lt. Governor, "What the hell, let's do it anyway." So, when I rode out to meet Tom, I carried his badge.

In celebration we rode back into Denver and put up for the night at the jail. I had a small house far out of town, but with the weather we decided the jail was best. Besides, we needed to catch the train first thing in the morning. Billy Patterson came by and hooped and hollered when we told him Tom had been reinstated. I reminded him it was only for the time being, but it didn't discourage him, he was happy and wanted to share a drink.

So, not wanting to put a damper on his spirits, I told him to get a bottle and bring it by. For Tom and I to walk into a saloon at this point in time did not seem like a good thing to do. It would appear as though we were flaunting the Lt. Governor's authority and I didn't want to do that. He and Tom both agreed so, we drank together in the jail until the bottle was dry.

We talked of old times, laughed at one another and ordered fried chicken from the restaurant. The whiskey warmed our blood and lightened our hearts. Time passed quickly and the early hours of morning crept up on us.

Outside a falling rain hammered against the roof of the jail. Billy was just about to leave when someone began pounding on the door. Still laughing at something Tom had said, Billy opened it. The shotgun blast caught him in the chest and threw him hard against the wall on the opposite side of the room. The horrible echo of the blast seemed to shake the entire building. Grabbing for our pistols Tom and I both dove for the floor, and as we hit, we could hear the faint sound of someone running away.

Tom rose almost immediately and ran after them.

Billy Patterson lay piled in a bloody heap on the floor near the wall. Kneeling, I checked for a pulse, there was none. Young Billy was dead.

Rising I walked to the open door and stared out into the cold winter darkness. The boardwalks were blanketed with ice and the falling rain arched against a fierce wind that howled for the friend who lay dead.

When Tom returned, he shrugged his disappointment. Whoever the shooter was they had vanished.

Moving around behind the desk I sat and poured a drink. This murder I knew was meant for Tom or myself, not Billy. Looking at him lying there on the floor I shook my head and downed the whiskey in my glass, then poured another, and one for Tom too.

We drank to Billy until my remaining deputies arrived for work. Once over the shock of his death I had them take his remains to the undertaker. When they carried him out, I felt emptiness… and a strong rekindle of my hate for Granger and Booker. Those bastards, I thought, right here in Denver. It was clear as the ice that covered the world outside the office door how powerful they were, with arms capable of reaching any distance.

Pulling on my coat, Tom asked where I was going. Looking into his face I told him. "To get Burroes out of bed."

Tom nodded. "Sounds like a good idea to me. Count me in."

When we left the jail rain was still falling. Above our heads the moon was partially visible and the solid sheet of ice that covered the ground shined with a glistening tone. The streets were slippery and dangerous, but I didn't care. Burroes's house was not that far, just two streets over. It was difficult walking, and it was cold. Twice I fell, but twice I picked myself up and continued. Then we were there, and I didn't knock. The door was locked so I kicked it open. The place was dark, but on the north side of the living room a curtain blew from the wind coming in through a broken window.

Tom found a lantern and lit it. Together we searched the house knowing only too well what we'd find, and what we thought, came true.

Burroes lay like Frankons, lifeless in his own bed. Only he had not been shot, his throat had been slashed. It was Granger's trademark; had he done this with his own hand? Was he himself in Denver?

Burroes had not been dead long. Blood still ran from the long cut in his throat so who ever killed him was here only minutes before us.

I couldn't wait to get back to Tucson and talk with Booker, and even more than that I wanted to stand face to face with Granger. The thought of sending a gram to the sheriff in Tucson crossed my mind, but I didn't know who I could trust. As far as I was concerned, Tom Wade and I were in this thing alone. Aside from Tom and the Lt. governor, Billy had been the only one I would have trusted. The reasoning now would have to be that everyone was out to get us.

Back at the jail we found a fresh pot of coffee brewing. Deputy Leon Brook was cleaning the last of Billy's blood off the floor. He looked up and asked sadly.

"Sheriff, who would do such a thing? Billy was always funnin' and bein' good to folks."

I walked over and put a hand on his shoulder. "It was Billy's time and he felt little pain. It was quick for him. I promise you Leon, whoever did this to him will answer to me."

"And me." Tom echoed.

By the time Leon was finished and left to walk rounds we had finished two cups of coffee. After pouring my third and building a smoke I sat down at the desk. Tom took out his watch; "it's "3:34, the train leaves in five and a half hours. I wish it were leaving right now."

"Me too," I told him, "But remember what you told me about patience. There's only you and me standing between Booker and an Indian War. We must be extra careful now, take everything slow and easy. If we die now there will be no stopping him."

Tom pulled up a chair and sat opposite me.

The rain continued to fall thickening the ice wherever it fell. The wind had picked up too and it swayed the signs hanging loose in front of buildings. For most of the people out there, sleep controlled their lives… no knowledge of the murder of a good man and the slaying of a bad.

Tomorrow they would know, for there would be gossip and rumors. But tonight, for me, the sleep they enjoyed could not happen. Inside I was a twisted mass of frustration. I struggled with patience, wishing the word never existed. I was filled with hate and hurt too. But like they say, 'for every bad there's a good'. And far from here, in the form of a beautiful woman good did exist…maybe love too… or so I hoped.

CHAPTER TWENTY-ONE

The return trip to Tucson seemed endless. I didn't know which I wanted more, to see Allison again or meet Charles Booker.

With all the killing going on I was worried for Allison and for good reason. The men we were dealing with were without feelings, cold-hearted killers who murdered cruelly and without remorse. It someone got in the way they took them out, and I felt if Booker suspected even his own sister of passing information on to us, she would be taken care of too.

I hoped the ledger was still at the Booker Ranch. Of course, Charles would not surrender it, so we would just have to walk in and take it. At the same time, I would hope Allison would come with us. We could all return to Denver and hopefully get everything cleared up, and those involved behind bars.

It sounded simple but Booker was much smarter than that, somehow, some way, he would complicate things. I didn't know how – only that he would.

The rules of the game were changing. For starters, the full legality of this thing was beginning to play a less important part. Since we now knew what the stakes were, there was more on the line beside justice in the legal sense. The lives of hundreds needed to be considered now, and there may not be time to do things by the letter of the law. If both Booker and Granger were dead, perhaps the whole plan would collapse and somehow, bottom line, I felt that if it came to that, the Lt. Governor would agree, although not publicly. If it failed, it would suit me fine, and Tom too no doubt.

The train arrived in Tucson beneath a hot, bright sun. In mid-afternoon we pulled to a stop at the depot, and I hoped Granger was there to greet us. Of course, he wasn't, and we made no bones about disembarking for all present to see.

There was no hurry in getting out to Booker's except of course to see Allison. I was sure he knew the same day we left Denver, that we were on our way. So, the place we headed was a restaurant to get a good meal. As soon as we were finished, we mounted and started for the ranch.

The place hadn't changed, nor the greeting. The cute kid with the dimples took the horses to the barn and Rubin met us at the porch. There was a strange look on his face though, and I knew something was wrong. When he gave his usual welcome there was trembling in his voice. I felt sorry for him suddenly and wished he worked for a man who could appreciate him.

We were led once again into the study just like before. Only this time there was no Allison to greet us, instead, behind the desk sat Charles Booker. He smiled the minute we were in front of him and rose from the chair in which he sat. He extended a hand in a phony gesture, but we didn't take it.

With a wave he told us to be seated. Once we were all comfortable, he spoke. His voice was soft and touched with a trace of aristocracy. His hair was neat and well-groomed with a touch of gray at the temples.

Like Allison, he was well tanned and the suit he wore was camel hair; the best money could buy. Opening his cigar box, he turned it our way and gestured, but again we declined.

Slightly irritated yet still smiling he said. "Well, finally we meet. Federal Marshal Steinberge and his right-hand man," Booker snickered, "or has he elevated from right hand man to your entire right-hand arm? I heard you lost a deputy in Denver. I'm terribly sorry. Denver must be a ghastly place. I understand he was gunned down in cold blood." Booker shook his head, "So shocking."

That was it. I started to leave my chair, but Tom grabbed my arm.

"Not now Arch."

Booker nodded his head in agreement. Looking directing at Tom he said.

"A most wise decision Mr. Wade. Had Marshal Steinberge left his chair…"

Tom cut him off. "The man behind us would have shot him."

Booker was smiling again.

"Yes, quite correct."

I looked over my shoulder and cursed my stupidity.

Tom told him, "The man is holding a Winchester, correct?"

"Right again, Mr. Wade."

"Tell me Mr. Booker," Tom added, "Which is faster to shoot twice, a rifle which needs to be levered or a pistol which you can simply fan repeatedly?"

Losing his smile, Booker replied.

"Why a pistol of course."

"Exactly," Tom told him, "You see, if your goon would have shot Marshal Steinberge, I would have pulled my .44 and put a bullet right between your eyes, and probably one between his, before he finished cocking another round into the chamber. So, I guess it was a wise move for all of us, wouldn't you agree?"

Booker's face went from tan to red. With an angered wave of his hand, he motioned for the man with the Winchester. "Come in here Buff and meet these gentlemen."

Through the doorway stepped the biggest man we'd ever seen. If he wasn't near seven feet, I'd have given my Badge to the town drunk. Just one of his hands equaled the size of both Tom and mine put together. If it were to come down to a man-to-man fist to cuff, it would be near impossible to win. This giant was ugly too. His hair was long like Tom's, but most of his natural teeth were missing – probably lost from walking into too many high tree branches.

When Booker introduced him, he said it with a touch of daring.

"Gentlemen. I'd like you to meet Buff, my personal bodyguard. In Italy he was a prized boxer. He's killed ten men in the ring and never lost."

Looking him up and down Tom smiled. "Tell me Buff, have you ever fought with a .44 round through the heart?"

Booker grinned. "I can assure you Mr. Wade Buff is also very good with a gun. And he never leaves my side."

"That's probably a good thing." I told him. Booker absorbed my words with a calculating stare. I let him get his share of wondering then added. "We were here a few days ago but you weren't home. We did meet your sister though. A nice lady, where is she now?"

Booker answered like he'd been waiting a long time for me to ask.

"It seems my sister was called away, someplace up north. Heaven knows where. I wouldn't wait for her return though; I understand she plans to stay a long while."

There was instant alarm and hatred. I wanted to grab him, but monster man was still holding the Winchester leveled on us. So, I forced a smile and I know it angered him.

"That's too bad." I edged him on, "I liked her, and she was a nice touch to the house here. Now the place will lack class."

That bothered him. He rose to his feet.

"Well gentlemen. Your time is up. I have things to do."

He yelled for Rubin. "My butler will show you to the door. Please refrain from visiting me again. If you do, I will consider it trespassing and have you shot on sight."

"That's interesting," I told him abruptly. "Will you shoot us yourself, or will Buff here do it for you?" I gave him a short laugh and finished with what I had to say. Ah, forgive me. How rude of me to think such a thing. Of course, you won't be the one, you're too cowardly to face another man yourself."

He stared at me with hate on his face, disliking my audacity. The man couldn't take his own medicine. As Rubin lead us out of the room, I stopped long enough to look back at him.

"You know, if we do come back Mr. Booker, you would be wise to shoot us on the spot, because next time, we will be coming for you."

Out on the porch Rubin hesitated as though he wanted to tell us something, but he remained silent. Maybe he felt now was not the time, and Booker was watching from his Den Window.

As Tom and I swung up into our saddles I asked him if he had ever seen anyone as big as Buff?

"Yeah once." He told me. "In a story book."

Reining south, we headed back to town were we stopped off at the saloon and drank a beer. There was no need to avoid contact any longer, besides, we were both ready for a fight should it happen.

While sitting at a table in the corner we talked. I was gravely concerned for Allison. Where was she? Booker knew, and I felt Rubin knew too. He probably overheard a conversation or saw something he wasn't supposed to. I wanted to talk with him but wasn't sure how. There would be no more riding out to the Booker ranch for social visits. Next time they would be waiting for us. No doubt with an army of armed men. Of course, Buff alone was an army.

Tom shared my concerns for Allison too. I shut out of my mind the worst of all possibilities. She was alive somewhere and I knew that she was waiting for me to come for her... wherever that may be.

When we had the beer finished, we left and took a room at the hotel. Dark was not far away, and when it came, I had determined to return to the Booker ranch and somehow talk with Rubin, however, that turned out unnecessary. At 9:31 there was a knock on our door. Standing to the side I opened it with pistol cocked. The little boy from the ranch was back again. He was smiling that dimpled smile, but when I pulled him into the room and quickly closed the door, it frightened him, and the smile disappeared.

"Sorry," I told him, "But a lot of people around here don't like us, and I wouldn't want you to get hurt.

After nodding his head, he gave Tom a wave and his smile came back with it. Then he looked back at me. "Sir, I have something for you." Reaching into his pocket he pulled out a folded piece of paper. "It's from Rubin. Said I was to get it to you right away."

After handing it to me the boy moved to the door.

"I must get back before Mr. Booker finds out I'm gone. He'll have me whipped if he does."

"Wait." I told him. He paused briefly and I slipped a silver dollar in his hand. His dimples showed up and he thanked me with an excited voice. Then out the door and down the hall he went.

Sitting on the edge of the bed I opened the letter. It was from Rubin all right. I read it aloud.

They took Ms. Booker

north to the Indians. Where I don't

know exactly. I think.

to the Sioux. She is with Mr. Granger.

I think they plan to trade her to them.

Please help her.

Rubin

Looking up at Tom I shook my head. "Some brother."

Tom rolled a cigarette and handed it to me. Then rolled one for himself and struck a match. I inhaled deep blowing the smoke toward the door. Tom's face grew sober.

"You ready to go get her?"

He put a hand on my shoulder compassionate for how I was feeling. Grasping his wrist. I gave him a nod. I couldn't speak.

CHAPTER TWENTY-TWO

We left Tucson beneath a sky cold and gray. A slim show of light etched through the eastern horizon as a warm sun rose patiently for its turn to light the world.

Everyone was saying north. But north to where? North covered a lot of territory.

We needed a clue, some small glimmer of specific area. Unfortunately, no one really knew but Booker. That was why we decided to pay him one more visit.

Looking into the sky I saw a handful of remaining stars. They were few, but still they represented the remaining darkness that would give us the cover we'd need to get into the house.

In a way I hoped Booker would oppose, draw on me and force my hand. To kill cold-blooded was not my style, but to put a bullet in him through self-defense would certainly cause me no unrest. Besides, my real reasons for going to his ranch were justified. I had every intention of finding out where they had taken Allison, and based upon the ledger she had shown me, I was putting him under arrest.

If the ledger was not there now, I would not be able to hold him long, but at least it would stir the pot and give me a little self-satisfaction. Besides, with Allison gone, her safety was no longer a weighing factor here.

Buff would be tough, but I would face that problem as fate unfolded.

A half-mile from the house we dismounted deciding to advance the rest of the way on foot. The night was quiet, and stillness swept the open ground. After removing our spurs, we grabbed our rifles and moved cautiously toward the house.

On the porch stood one guard. He held a Winchester across his arms and stood motionless, staring out into the darkness. There was another at the back, near the steps and he too held a rifle and stood gazing.

It was decided Tom would take the man in front and I the one in the back. While moving cautiously toward the side of the house, we passed a huge wood pile where each of us took a small piece in hand. Then moving on, we worked our way up until we stood with our backs against the side of the house. After motioning with a finger, we started for our respective corners.

Once there, we each tossed our wood pieces into the darkness in front of our man. Each, almost simultaneously, cocked their Winchester and started for the noise. My man walked straight out at half a crouch. Quietly, I began slipping up behind him, then he heard me. Turning in a second's time, his rifle barrel pulled around leveled at me, gut high.

There was no time for a silent strike with the pistol butt, so I dove to the right an instant before the Winchester went off. Firing twice as I dove, I saw him fall with the rifle spilling from his hands. I assumed Tom had been successful, for I heard nothing from the front of the house. Of course, it really didn't matter now, my shots would wake everyone anyway.

Rising to my feet, I scrambled to the back door and peered in. I saw no one. The door was locked so I broke it open with my shoulder. It slammed loud against the wall, but I didn't care. Scurrying across the kitchen, I pressed myself tight against the wall near the hallway entrance.

There was a short-lived noise at the other end of the house somewhere, and I guessed it to be Tom coming in through the front door. Upstairs footsteps scampered across the wood floor. Probably Buff and Booker, maybe Rubin too.

The hallway was dark and the parlor too at the far end. Staying low I stared down the hall, hugging the wall tight. It was important I get to the other end, for there was the stairway down which Buff and Booker would come. The noise upstairs eventually fell silent.

Senses tuned; I focused mainly on the area at the end of the hallway. I still had no idea where Tom was, but in my mind, I pictured Buff to be standing at the head of the stairs…waiting.

The shadowed house was silent and cold as a stone mortuary. The parlor ahead was black, but through the window I could see that the sky was beginning to lighten considerably. In only minutes there would be light everywhere. Once at the far end of the hallway, I waited.

Then came the sound of something scraping against the floor in a room off the parlor. A few seconds later, in that same room, someone struck a match, and I heard the squeak of a lantern being lit. There was a sudden burst of bright light and nervously I waited as the person holding the lamp moved through that room toward the parlor door.

Unsure of what was going on, I watched the concentration of light grow brighter as it moved toward me… and then they were there. The light filled the parlor, and I got a clear look at the man holding the lantern.

As he held it slightly above his head, below it I saw Tom wearing an apologetic look. Behind him holding a rifle to Tom's back Buff smiled. He was so much taller that the area around his head and shoulders appeared hazy. Not happy with the situation I frowned, and when Booker laughed from the head of the stairs I couldn't help it, I said it out loud, "Shit."

Booker laughed. 'Yes Marshal Steinberge, the word is most appropriate. You seem to be up to your ears in it." He then paused and went on, always remaining in the shadows.

"Now, drop your gun or I shall order Buff to kill Mr. Wade. I have a gun pointed at you too, so please be reasonable."

What could I do? Throwing down my pistol, we all listened as it fell loud against the hardwood floor. Booker descended the stairs then, followed by Rubin who he ordered to build a fire.

When Booker reached the bottom, he came straight to where I stood and picked up my .44. He cocked it, put the barrel to my head and grinned.

I stared at him coldly. "Well." I told him.

"Well what Marshal?" He said with a widening contemptuous grin.

"Do you or don't you have the balls?"

He grew sober for an instant and I thought I saw his trigger finger move slightly. Then he burst into laughter.

"Oh Marshal Steinberge, you do so amuse me. But do not underestimate my resolve. I have every intention of killing you, but first I'd like to share with you a little 'live' entertainment. I want to see what kind of man your deputy is?"

I looked from him to Tom, then back.

"What are you talking about Booker?"

"A fight Marshal, fist to fist, man to man. Your righthand man against my righthand man, Buff."

"Bullshit Booker". I told him with no hesitation. That's no match. It's murder."

"Perhaps, but at the moment it is I who is calling the shots, so I say they fight."

Rubin had the fire going now and the room was filled with light. Outside the sun was up and even more light poured in through the windows. Another new day had been born to the earth, but for Tom it could very easily be the last. I needed to do something, and it was obvious my options were limited. I looked at the gun in Booker's hand, then told him with a flippant smile.

"I was right, wasn't I?"

"About what?" The puzzlement I had hoped for showed in Booker's eyes.

"Right about what?" Booker asked again.

"About you. You really are a coward, a yellow ballless coward. Does Buff do all your fighting for you? Why don't you and I have it out, right here and now. Instead of the giant and the ant, you and me, the U S Marshal and no Balls Booker?"

Booker studied my face. Our eyes were locked. He calculated his chances. I was sure he was thinking that beating me would be a trophy to covet. Killing me in cold blood would be easy, but to beat me in a fair fight would bring him insurmountable satisfaction at the table of his rich fellow poker players.

Tom caught on and spoke up.

"Yeah Booker. You fight the Marshal, then when he's ruined your arrogant face and your cold blood covers the floor, I'll rip your toothless gorilla here, apart." Tom gestured with a pointed thumb over his shoulder toward Buff.

Booker was unsure now. We had ruffled his pride, poked him where it hurt. He was a man use to having his own way, and now for that to happen he was being forced to except things on someone else's terms. I continued to egg him on.

"Go ahead. Pull the trigger on my own gun and kill me. Make it easy. But remember, if I die by your murdering me in cold blood, and not in a fair fight, I may be dead, but I will also be the better man. And you'll have to live with that thought the rest of your life.

There was a strain on his face. His jaw muscles were tight, and his fingers milked the handle of the pistol he held pointed at me. There was no doubt, if brains were made of wood smoke would be coming out of his ears.

Booker was thinking and the wheels in his head turning. But there was no fear in his face. This man led a rich aristocratic life, but I'd bet my badge he had had his share of fights and more than once tasted his own blood. He would be no one to underestimate.

A smile suddenly appeared on his lips then and he lowered the gun. We continued to stare and for some time there was silence. Then he broke it.

"Then so be it, Marshal Steinberge. We shall fight. But not like animals. We shall have a duel. Out of doors, beneath the sky. Just you and I, each with a single shot pistol, back-to-back – ten paces then turn and fire. One shall live and the other die. Let me assure you though, my ancestors were duelers, my father and his father before him, and none, I might add, have ever lost. A Booker just don't lose. We have been winners for centuries. Today, you're dying by my gun, shall add to family tradition."

He turned to Rubin standing quietly by the fire.

"Bring me my dueling pistols."

Rubin hesitated and started to speak, but Booker cut him off.

"Damn you nigger!" I didn't ask you to speak, I told you to go get my dueling pistols. Now go!"

Rubin left immediately and I was sure he left embarrassed and humiliated. Booker turned to face me again.

"I apologize for my servant."

"No," I said irritated, "it is Rubin who should apologize for you. You truly are a bastard."

Booker studied me. Confused as to why I would side with a lowly servant over a man of money and means. I did not give him a reply, my smirk and shaking head said what I had to say.

Within a few seconds Rubin returned with a leather case which Booker took from his hands. He then turned and walked outside. With a pointed rifle Buff motioned for us to follow. Rubin remained in the house.

The sky was clear. A bright sun set high above now and there would be no difficulty in seeing a target. Booker opened the case and turned it my way.

Two silverplated, single shot percussion pistols with ivory grips lay side by side, each with its own loading necessities.

"Choose Mr. Steinberge", Booker said, "Both are of excellent quality." There was both pride and arrogance in his voice, "And feel free to load your own, I shall do the same to mine."

Booker turned to speak to Rubin, but he was not there. Irritated once again, he carried the pistol case to the porch and set it down. When he was loaded himself, he returned to where I stood.

"Shall we?"

Together we turned back-to-back and raised the pistols shoulder high.

Booker looked over at Tom.

"Mr. Wade, would you be so kind as to count for us."

Tom looked my way, and I gave him a wink. Then he looked back to Booker.

"Certainly. I'd love to count the last ten steps of your life."

Booker made a bored expression, saying. "Please Mr. Wade, do cease with the trivial discourtesies and just count."

I looked at Tom one more time and he was grinning. My wink must have convinced him of my confidence to win. I only wished it had done the same for me.

The count began and we started stepping out.

One… Two… Three…

I thought about the statement Booker had made concerning ancestors and how they never lost, and what kind of a shot he was? I wondered too if he'd cheat and turn early, and what Tom would do if Booker's bullet took me out?

With the colt I was a good shot, but with a percussion pistol I had never fired before, I didn't know. During my childhood I had hunted with an old musket rifle, but that didn't count.

Seven… Eight…

If I killed Booker - the only person to know of Allison's whereabouts - I might never find her again. But this was a duel to the finish, one of life or death. It was one thing at a time and right now what mattered was how straight I could shoot.

TEN!

It all seemed to happen in slow motion. Our bodies turned; arms stretched, and guns pointed outward. There was one loud crack and I saw smoke belch from the barrel of Booker's gun. Perhaps a fraction of a second, but no more, and I fired too, feeling Booker's ball whiz past my ear. I felt the air from its closeness.

My own shot tore into Charles Booker's chest. As he fell, Tom spun around and grabbed for the barrel of Buff's rifle. It went off in the air and they began to struggle. But the scrape lasted only a short time. There came a second shot in the air and this time if came from none of us.

Rubin stood Ton the porch holding a double barrel shotgun – one of its barrels still smoking. I was glad to hear his voice.

"You all stop this fighting. Buff, you drop that rifle and step over here near me so I can keep an eye on you. If you try anything at all I swear I will kill you."

Big Buff did as he was told. Rubin turned my way.

"Mr. Steinberge, I am truly sorry I didn't do something sooner. I guess I was just too afraid."

"You did fine Rubin." I said warmly. "You did just fine,"

Moving to Booker I kneeled at his side. He was staring up at me with open eyes, but I knew not for long. There was blood in his mouth and the front of his shirt was soaked with it too. Grabbing his shoulder, I asked.

"Allison. Where is Granger taking her?"

He gripped my wrist and spoke, his voice gargled with the blood filling his throat.

"You beat me."

There was urgency in my voice. "Booker, where have they taken Allison?"

He coughed and blood bubbled out, but he managed to say; "David is taking her to Victorio."

"Why in God's name to him? He'll enslave her."

Booker tried for one last smile, his once white teeth glistening with red.

"My dear sister…" gasping in pain he continued, "Has always been a thing of desire to him."

"She's your sister for God's sake." I said.

Booker's grip was beginning to lighten. "Victorio is a savage yes, but a friend. A man who takes what he wants, and I needed him. Allison was just in the way, always in the way. She…".

That was Booker's last word. His eyes quit blinking and he was dead.

Rising to my feet I pulled my hat from my head and ran my fingers through my hair, wondering. He had said Victorio was someone he needed. Needed for what?

Placing my hat back on my head I turned to Tom. "Well, we know more than we did."

Rubin spoke up from the porch.

"Mr. Steinberge. Who is this Victorio?"

I looked at him, my voice edged with a trace of hopelessness I couldn't hide.

"Rubin. Victorio is the devil himself in an Indian's body".

CHAPTER TWENTY-THREE

After sending Buff away for good with nothing but his horse and clothes, we went back into the house. While Tom and I headed for the study, Rubin went to the barn to hitch up a wagon in which to take Booker's body into town.

We rummaged through the desk and found the ledger exactly where Allison had put it, but I wasn't satisfied. I had a feeling there was more, I just didn't know where. We checked under tables, behind books, in closets and everywhere we thought something of value might be hidden.

Then behind a painting of the Colorado Rockies we found Booker's safe. It was locked, but as we had hoped, Rubin knew the combination. It was like striking gold. There was a duplicate ledger as I had suspected. There were several letters from the man called Matt and this time two of them had a return address.

We also found a small cloth bag with interesting contents. When we dumped it out on the desktop, gold, diamonds, rubies and sapphires tumbled out. Also, in the safe, we found an ancient ceremonial mask of some sort fashioned with turquoise, along with a small stone statue which Rubin had heard Booker brag about. It was the statue of Ehécatl, the wind God of the Aztecs. No doubt it was priceless.

With all the items laid out on the desk, I sat down and stared at them. Was there a connection between Booker, the uprisings and these artifacts? Taking the two letters from the man called Matt, I glanced at the return addresses. Both were from Mexico City. What was Matt doing there? Perhaps arranging for guns to be brought across the border. But why so far away? Surely gun purchasing arrangements could be made closer to home. I opened one of the letters and read it to myself.

Charles,

Things going splendidly here. Three more articles
are on their way. I tell you Charles,
you won't believe your eyes.
They are magnificent.
Arrangements have been made at this end.
All is well. But Vic is growing more discontented
with each day. Guns do not seem to be enough anymore.
I shudder to think of what will happen if we lose him,
or worse, his man here. Will meet with Vic on Monday.
He will have the items with him. Please ensure
the rifles are on time. See you in Kanob on Tuesday
for pick-up.

Matt

After handing the letter to Tom, I leaned back in the chair and gave it some thought.

It appeared that Matt was some sort of middleman. After rolling a cigarette I took one draw and sat straight up. Of course! It was so simple. A connection in Mexico City was stealing priceless artifacts, giving them to this Matt, who in return took them and made arrangements for them to be taken somewhere near the border. Then Victorio would pick them up and bring them into the country as only he could do freely with no one the wiser. In exchange for artifacts worth millions, Booker gave him guns.

According to the letter, the connection in Mexico was a friend to Victorio and probably stole for his cause. Or, with Mexico being as downtrodden as it was, Booker's man Matt may have been paying pennies for these treasures. But nevertheless, had he not been stopped, Charles Booker would have stolen the country of Mexico blind. I did wonder though, just how much of this Granger knew about? Probably very little.

The second letter was old by about four months. Its contents mentioned a pickup again, also in Kanob. Its envelope was dated November 23. Nearly two months ago. Leaning back in the chair again, I took another on my cigarette.

Kanob was north, just to the Utah line. What if Granger was going there with Allison, to meet up with Matt and Victorio? Today was Tuesday. It could just be that this coming Monday was the day talked about in the letter. Then again, it could have been last Monday. It was a shot in the dark but at least it was a shot. If we caught a train north, we could be there by the weekend.

Tom handed me back the letter and I placed it in the envelope.

"Well?" He asked. "What do you think?"

Giving him a sober look, I said. "Why not You may find who you're looking for and I may find who I'm looking for."

Tom nodded. "Arch, I've got a good feeling about this."

I hoped he was right. If not, and Kanob turned out a mistake I could lose Allison forever.

By 10:30 we were back on the train. If nothing else I thought, we were certainly doing our share in supporting the railroad, even if it was the city of Denver's money.

The trek across Arizona was miserable. Even with the windows open the coach was unbearably hot. Outside the temperature must have been a hundred or more and as always, the train rocked and vibrated to an irritable degree.

In my heart I feared greatly for Allison. It was bad enough she was with Granger, but Victorio? He was a warrior to be reckoned with. For countless months now the Army had been chasing him across Arizona and New Mexico in hot pursuit. But they always failed to catch him. He and his small band of Mescaleros were invincible. They would push their ponies until they dropped, kill and eat them, then continue while the soldier's horses dredged along, carrying an extra hundred pounds of military gear. When they dropped, progress was stopped.

The calvary was just no match for Victorio. This man not only won great victories against the United States Army, but he frequently raided into Mexico and beat the Federalies as well. One lone warrior and a small band of followers against the Armies of two countries and neither one, nor the two combined could catch him.

Sighing, I leaned my head against the back of the seat and pulled my hat over my eyes. VICTORIO. If he got his hands on Allison before I did it would take an act short of a miracle to get her back. With Booker out of the picture it could just be that the gun running problem would come to an end. I doubted that Granger had the connections to pick up the ball and continue the game. He was good at pushing his weight around and giving orders to brainless men, but without brother Charles's know how and organization he was like a cook on a trail drive without a chuck wagon. Yet nevertheless things were beginning to drag on and I wanted them ended.

Yawning, I let my head roll with the movement of the train.

Once Granger was apprehended and we had Allison back, this whole mess could be cleared up. I wanted to return to Denver and put my life back on kilter. Of course, if Allison happened to feel the same then…

The sudden jerk of the train nearly threw me out of my seat. We were making an emergency stop and amidst the yelling of the passengers, I realized that I had been asleep.

The whistle blew repeatedly and finally the train halted to a complete stop. Like everyone else on board, we had no idea what was going on.

Outside the sun was setting and the desert lay obscured in a dim, hazy light.

Pulling my watch, I read 6:23 p.m. Trying to unclog the sleep from my brain and figure out what was going on, I caught a quick glimpse of two riders galloping past the coach windows toward the rear of the train. The one on the opposite side went by heading toward the front. I looked at Tom and started to speak when the coach door behind us flung open and a man wearing a red bandana over his face stepped in. There was a shotgun in his hands, and it was pointed down the aisle for quick movement to either side. When he shouted at us his voice was slightly muffled, but the orders were clear.

"Everybody put up your hands. Any of you gents want to be heroes, stand up now so I can kill you and get it over with. Otherwise just sit with your mouths shut and hands in the air."

There were nineteen people on the train, fourteen were men. But men or women, 38 arms were a lot for one man to watch, even with a scatter gun for back up.

Then through the door at the opposite end of the coach a second man stepped in; this one holding a rifle and he too had his face covered.

The first man yelled across the now silent coach at him, his voice slightly irritated.

"Where the hell have you been? We were supposed to bust through at the same time."

"Sorry Hank."

Hank cursed. "Shut up you idiot." He was flat irritated now. "Take off your hat and gather up the money in it. If they won't give it to you, stand them up and I'll put a hole in their back. Now do it." At that the second man pulled off his hat and began doing what he had been told.

Inside the coach the evening shadows were thick, and it was getting hard to see. Motioning to the conductor with the barrel of his shotgun, the first man in ordered him to light the lanterns. So doing as ordered the conductor brought them one by one to life starting in the front and working back. The coach brightened in slow, overlapping sections. Using my eyes, I motioned for Tom to concentrate his attention on the man with the hat.

Earlier, I had spotted three riders outside. Time had been too short for any of them to be the man nearest us. He had come through the door at almost the same instant the men had rode past. The late arrival however was different, he in fact could easily have one, and if he was, then I could account for four men – two in and two outside somewhere. The two outside had probably split, one to the engineer and the other to the caboose to search for a strong box and rummage through personal belongings. If we were going to make a move it needed to be done while they were separated.

Watching the shot gunned guard out of the corner of my eye, waited for an opportunity to lower my right arm without him noticing. Every minute or so, he'd nervously glance out the windows on either side of the train. The man with the collection hat and Winchester was working his way up quickly. I wasn't exactly sure how to play the hand, but I wanted it to be right. Scatter guns make a nasty hole in a man's body.

The man looked out the window and down came my arm. His eyes were back in a second, but he didn't notice one arm missing. We were lucky the coach was full. Easing my gun out, I held it across my lap. The man with the hat was two seats away. He held the Winchester down by his side with his free hand, so both hands were occupied. One last time I motioned toward him with my eyes and Tom acknowledged.

Then he was there, and his eyes saw my gun. His mouth opened to yell, but Tom was fast, he was out of his seat and spinning him around about the time the yell made it out of his throat. It all happened in seconds. So fast in fact no one else on board realized what was happening until the scatter gun exploded with deafening sound. The blast caught the man with the hat square in the back and the force knocked both Tom and him to the floor in the aisle.

Now there were screams and panic from the passengers. The colt in my hand erupted twice and both bullets took the gunman in the chest. His body hurtled backward out through the door on to the platform. Tom scrambled to his feet and came up with his gun in his hand. He ran for the far door, yelling for everyone to get down between the seats. There was a mad scramble and in seconds they were all out of sight.

At the back door I crouched. In front of me was the cattle car and behind it the caboose where I was sure at least one man was now scrambling to get to his horse. I heard a faint whinny and a man yell git, then came the pounding of horse hoofs. He was riding toward me along the train. Ten seconds, no more, and he'd be in front of me – an easy target. I waited patiently. The hoof beats grew louder, sounding like muffled thunder. There wasn't a lot of light left outside... but enough. There were two horses but only one rider. I fired my shot and my target fell from the saddle. Puzzled, I wondered why the extra horse? Was he bringing it for one of the men in our coach?

Then it dawned and I looked up. He was on top of the cattle car at the edge looking down, right at me.

"Shit." I dove to the right the instant he fired, and the bullet took a chunk out of my boot heel. Then came a second shot and I waited for the bullet to tear into my body – but I never felt it. Glancing up I saw the man's body fall from the top of the car. Tom stood in the doorway behind me, smiling. Letting out a long sigh, I sat up and wrapped my arms around my knees.

"Thanks." I told him.

Tom winked. "You're welcome."

CHAPTER TWENTY-FOUR

The terrain around Kanob was mountainous with miles and miles of places to hide. There were high plateaus with deep ravines and monster cliffs. Endless trails led in all directions and often dead-ended. If someonc wanted to hold a secretive rendezvous, Kanob Utah was ideal.

Tom and I both had been through the area a few times over the years, and knew only too well that without at least a whisper of direction, we may as well be looking for a a string of hay in a haystack.

We also knew that if Victorio was able to slip through the tight net of the U.S. and Mexican armies-our chances of finding him would be next to impossible. But as they say, so long as you believe there's hope… then there is.

Kanob was small. A few buildings, a handful of scattered ranches about, and little else. The train had gone only as far as flagstaff, so we rode the rest of the way on horseback.

As we ambled in, we studied the town with anxious eyes. It was a one street affair with a single saloon, a blacksmith, a small store, stable and a handful of private houses. The only hotel was more of a boarding house. Finding out information here should not prove too difficult.

The saloon was a large, one room affair. A short bar, seven unmatching tables and a well-worn piano. The tender was a medium sized guy with a mop of red hair and a wide, thick mustache curled at the ends. It was obvious he had spent a lot of time on it and took great pride with it. In addition to the bartender, and ourselves only one other man was present.

A Mexican in a sombrero and single pistol belt across his chest, sat alone at a table nursing a bottle of whiskey. I couldn't see his face for the brim of his hat, but I knew he was watching us.

Our boot heels clicked against the floor as we crossed to the bar. Once there, we each ordered a beer and when the tender returned with them, I started a conversation. "How's business? The bartender shrugged his shoulders and gave me a bored look. "Slow." He replied.

Taking out my makings, I diligently rolled a cigarette. "Too bad about business." I told the keep, "No business, no money". After pausing a moment, I added. "But maybe we can be of some help." His interest picked up although I felt like maybe it was more curiosity.

"My friend and I are looking for some people".

Pulling out the sketch of Granger, I handed it to him. "This man might also have a woman with him." The tender looked the drawing over closely then handed it back. "Why are you looking for him? You fellows' bounty hunters?"

He glanced over at Tom then back at me waiting for the answer.

"No," we're not bounties." Pulling my vest out of the way I let him see the badge and waited for him to read United States Marshal.

" The man is a killer," I told him "And the woman I mentioned was abducted by him."

He leaned on the bar. "Is there a reward? "No," I said slightly irritated, "but there's twenty dollars in it for you if you can tell me something." There was a long pause as he studied the situation. The man knew something, and I wanted to know what, so I waited patiently.

Tom took a sip of beer then casually turned his body so he could watch the Mexican.

The tender was our big break, and we couldn't afford not to know what information he had. A good two minutes passed before he opened, "Yeah. I've seen this man. Been in here lots. Always orders whiskey. Has three bouts, never more, then leaves. I'll tell ya; he's a horse's ass twice over. I believe he could kill ya while eaten dinner and never miss a bite.

Taking a sip of beer, I edged him on. "Yep, that's him. When did you see him last?

The tender made a face and glanced up at the ceiling. "Been weeks. Maybe a couple months or so."

I took another sip and the voice behind us took me by surprise.

"Amigo. I think I have seen this man you're looking for-and with him was a woman. Also, six men."

Turning from the bar, I looked across the room at the lone Mexican sipping his whiskey.

"How long ago?"

"It was but a day ago."

"Where?" He motioned with his head, "Near here. In the hills to the north."

I couldn't believe what I was hearing. Finally, things seemed to be going our way again.

Leaving the bar, I crossed to where he sat and joined him at his table. Tom remained at the bar-watching. "There's no reward," I told him, "But I will pay you twenty dollars same as the tender, and believe me, you've already earned most of it."

The Mexican laughed. His teeth were white and even, unlike so many of his kind. In fact, he himself was clean and well groomed. But his face and hands were covered with little red welts-like bites. They were obvious, but I gave him the courtesy of not starting and not asking.

"Senor," he went on. "It is not money I seek for this information. I wish to ride with you and help hunt this man down. He is a bad one and poisons our world. Only his death can be the cure."

I sat back in my chair and looked deep into the Mexicans eyes. Like Tom, they held hate, a drive for revenge. I wanted to know why, but I didn't ask. If he wanted to tell me, it would be in his own time. I wondered too, just who he was. This man had pride and a certain way about him. Though quiet in nature, he had that air of warning - that awareness that some men have - radiating the message to steer clear, and if you couldn't, then you'd best be civil.

I showed him the drawing and he gave a positive nod. We talked a long while. He had been in the hills gathering horses for the rancher he worked for, he and another, a friend. They had come upon Granger and his crew unexpectedly. The reception they received was not what they had expected. The friend was murdered and he himself had been stripped, covered with honey and staked to the ground over an ant hill. He called himself Pocko and I liked him.

During our conversation he had described Allison perfectly and told me she had looked unharmed. Her hands had been bound at their camp; she had given Granger a lashing for what they were doing to him, but Granger only laughed and ordered her gagged.

While we talked, other men had begun to drift into the saloon. The tender had greeted each with a friendly welcome, so I figured them all to be locals.

Outside, evening shadows were gathering in the street. We talked on for some time and before we had finished, the entire saloon had grown quite busy. The bar filled up and all the tables were taken. A lone saloon girl had come in and began serving drinks. A piano player showed up too.

By the time Pocko's bottle went dry, we had agreed to meet at first light and ride together to the spot where Granger was camping. I wanted to go now and so did Tom, but I respected this man's rights, and besides, I was learning too well the meaning of patience.

At the bar Tom had learned that a well-dressed gentleman had stopped in earlier for a beer. That this man too, according to the tender, had been in several times before in the months past. He was presently checked in at the boarding house down the street and especially interesting to us was the man's name . . . Matt Grimes.

Before we left, I laid the bartender's money in front of him. He picked it up and put it in his pocket. As we left the bar he shouted after us. "Next time you're in the first beer is on me."

We stepped out into a surprisingly warm night. The sky was full of stars and a full moon hung luminous above our heads.

Damn we were so close. I wanted to move, and I wanted to move now. Somewhere beyond town a coyote called out into the night and for some reason I thought of Victorio.

Untying Gertrude she whinnied and stomped her foot on the ground. She was hungry and telling me she wanted a stable for the night. As I unhitched her, I patted her neck. "Ok old girl. Let's go to the livery."

I was tired too, but for me there would be no sleep. Allison and Granger were close, and close too, was an end to all of this. It was our belief Matt Grimes had no idea who we were, or that Charles Booker was dead.

After putting the horses up for the night, we walked to the boarding house where fortunately we were able to get a room. We discovered that Matt was just down the hall in room 103, and by now, sound asleep.

After putting our gear away, we slipped out and went to his room. His door was not locked, so after a quick look over our shoulder, we slipped in. It was dark inside, but all the rooms were pretty much the same, so I just felt along the wall to the dresser and found the lamp.

Lighting it, I grabbed it and we made our way to sleepy Matt. The light woke him, and he squinted up at Tom, "Hey, what the . . ."

Tom slipped a hand over his mouth and whispered. "Keep your mouth shut, answer our questions and you won't get hurt. Got it?"

Grimes nodded and mumbled the word yes. But just to be safe and make sure he understood, I drew my pistol and laid it on the footboard of his bed. Tom sat down beside him and removed his hand.

"Now that we understand each other we can get on with business." He told him.

As was suspected, Matt Grimes had no idea who we were and constantly eyed my gun. He was afraid and that was the way we wanted it.

Tom continued. "We know why you're here so don't try and blow smoke in our ear. My partner and I want Granger, and we want him bad. He has Allison Booker with him, and we want her too. The gentleman at the foot of your bed is a United States Marshall,"

I grinned at him and let him see my badge then Tom went on. "We know about Mexico City, the priceless artifacts, your alliance with Victorio and the guns . . . quite frankly Mr. Grimes you're in a pile of horse manure up to your ears. Now, do you have anything to say for yourself?"

Grimes was a little worm of a guy with big ears. He looked from my gun to my face then over at Tom. "Oh gees, OH gees, OH GEES!" was all he could get out. Tom grew a little irritated and grabbed him by the front of his bed shirt pulling his skinny little body to a sitting position on the bed. "Look," Tom told him, "The Marshall and I don't have time to sit and listen to anything except the facts, so start talking."

Grimes cleared his throat.

"Oh gees, I . . . I don't know where to start."

"Start with telling us the place you're meeting Granger and Victorio." Tom was growing impatient. "Look Grimes," he said, "this little organization you and Booker had going is over, as a matter of fact I'll tell you right now . . . Booker is dead."

There was a look of disbelief on Grimes' face, and he turned white.

"Oh gees, how?"

I spoke up then. "I killed him. I shot him." Grimes looked over at me, then again down at the gun beside me. "OH GEES." Tom began rolling a cigarette and talked as he worked.

"You know, if you cooperate with us, we just might put in a good word for you with the judge when you go to trial, who knows, you might even get out of going to jail."

Grimes bit at his lower lip. He was thinking about his future. "OK, OK I'll tell you." He said finally. "There's a place east of here on the other side of the river, at the Big Rock Bridge. We're meeting tomorrow afternoon."

"Will everyone be there?"

"Yes."

"What about Allison Booker?"

"Her too, and Victorio. He will never let you ride away though, especially with Allison. He's got a thing for her, and Charles has given her to him."

I couldn't help myself, "You pathetic little kiss ass! You would have gone along with it, wouldn't you? Delivering an innocent woman into the hands of an animal like Victorio . . . all for the want of MONEY. You're as deranged as Booker was."

Grimes looked over at Tom and grabbed his arm. "You will help me, won't you? I mean, speak up for me at the trial. You Promised." There were almost tears in his eyes. Tom grabbed his hand and removed it from his arm, then rose saying. "You stay right here in town until we get back. When we do, we'll all return to Denver and get everything cleared up. You try sneaking away and we'll hunt you down, so be a nice little man and stay put."

Tom moved to the door and opened it while I blew out the lantern. The room grew dark again and we left Matt Grimes to his own thoughts. As I closed his door behind me, I heard him mumble . . . "Oh Gees."

Once in our own room, I took a chair and Tom stretched out on the bed. We didn't light the lantern. Moonlight shined in through the window with light enough to see one another. Tom built a cigarette and took a draw. He spoke as he exhaled.

"You think Grimes is telling the truth about tomorrow?"

"I don't know. If he isn't, I'll choke him."

"I know the place he's talking about" Tom added, "It is ideal for a secret meeting. Lots of places to hide."

Tom and I both knew the place. It was a land of enchantment. A splendid wilderness dressed in colorful rock formations of all shapes and sizes. But the one Grimes talked about was a natural rock bridge honed by the ice age thousands of years ago. It stood over three hundred feet into the sky and spanned at almost the same distance. There was a stream bed beneath it that twisted its way through a canyon floor that turned and curved in every direction. Tom was right too, there were a lot of places to hide. There would be no room for error tomorrow and having Pocko along as an extra gun would certainly help.

When Tom's cigarette was finished, he laid his head on his pillow and drifted off. His breathing was soft and even. Outside the window the stars seemed even brighter than earlier. Perhaps it was a sign, an omen of good fortune. Maybe tomorrow would bring the end to it all.

My thinking turned to Allison. What was she doing? How were they treating her? I wanted her back and would stop at nothing. This time, I would have my way. Thinking about the night we had spent together; a warm smile came to my face. Allison Booker was clearly a wonderful woman. She was a lady, not in the same sense as Sally. Sally was a different case; she enjoyed her work at Leeann's and had no desire to do something different. I understood and respected her feelings, and unlike many others in Denver, I still respected her.

Rolling a smoke, I struck a match, but cupped the light in my hand. As I shook the match out, I paused a moment listening. Outside in the hallway there had been a faint noise and I had barely picked it up. Unsure of what it was, I pulled my gun in my hand and moved quietly to the door. Then easing it open I looked out. Shadows were thick in many places; a man could be hiding, and I'd never see him. There was no other sound, so I closed the door and put the chair underneath the handle. Maybe it was just me.

I finished my cigarette then laid down staring into the dark ceiling. I wanted peace of mind no one was outside our door, and listening was the only safe answer.   Folding my arms behind my head, I looked out through the window. I could see the moon and stars around it. It was a beautiful night in Kanob, Utah, but I would much rather have been in Denver… with Allison. When Tom shook my shoulder, it startled me, and I came off the bed in a hurry. "Jumpy this morning, are we?" He said as if it were funny.

Though blurry and squinty eyes, I could make out the faint smile on his face. The lantern light coming from the dresser was bright. Outside the sky was still dark and starry, but I could tell that first light was not far away. "Were you planning to sleep till noon?" Tom went on.

"No." I said with a frown.

"Good." He smiled a little wider, "I certainly wouldn't want to keep Granger waiting, and you have a date with a lady remember?"

With that, I returned his smile. He continued, "You know Arch, it just might be a good idea to take our skinny little friend down the hall with us, know that I mean?"

"Fine with me," I told him. "Why don't you go get him while I wash up a little."

After strapping on his gun belt, Tom left. I splashed water on my face and tried to wake up. There was no time to shave, although I would have liked too.

While drying my face with a towel, Tom returned. There was concern in his voice and he was alone.

"Guess what."

I didn't want to ask. But I did.

"What?"

Tom motioned with his index finger for me to follow him. Still holding the towel, I followed him down the hall into Matt Grimes' room. Tom had lit the lantern, so the room was clear to see. The skinny little guy with the big ears lay quiet in his bed. His throat had been cut. I looked at Tom. One word… "CRAP".

CHAPTER TWENTY-FIVE

Body turned over to the Sheriff, we walked to the livery and saddled our horses. Pocko joined us there and together we rode out. By the time we were out of sight of the town, the sun was above us and the light of day was everywhere. It was a clear sky, and the morning air was warm. At least the final showdown was going to take place on a beautiful day.

Pocko turned north and we followed. Around eight-thirty we came upon the spot where Granger's camp had been. The cold remains of a cooking fire were there and not far from it was the ant hill where they had tied Pocko. The insects had already started to rebuild the hill and he went over to it and kicked it apart with his boot, cursing in Mexican as he did.

Obviously, Granger and the others had moved on to the stone bridge in preparation for the rendezvous. We hadn't asked Grimes about the guns since the letters from him had mentioned the need of them being delivered on time. Probably they were with Granger and his men. We had no idea how many followers would be with Victorio. Granger had six... at least six that we knew of. There would be no surprising them either, Grimes' murder had proven they knew we were here. Once again it appeared they had the upper hand.

Moving east, we made our way to the Colorado river. Going was slow since much of our travel was on solid rock. The horses' hoofs clicked against the hard surface and above us the sun grew higher in the sky, throwing down more heat. It would be a hot, torturous day, but that was the least of our worries; and none of it was to my liking.

First there was Granger himself . . . ruthless, a killer, a man void of any compassion, and with him were others; brainless followers probably as merciless as he.   Secondly, there was Victorio, a devil in his own right and worse than Granger ever dreamed of being. Just how many followers rode with him we had no way of knowing. At last count by the United States Army, well over sixty. Then there was Allison, caught in the middle, an innocent victim in a hopeless situation. If we failed, I knew well what would become of her; a harsh life enslaved to Victorio; she would be better off dead. All that I really knew was that we were three guns against many!

The smart thing to do would be to turn around and wait until after the rendezvous, catch Granger and his men alone. At least the odds would be a bit more favorable. However, that would leave Victorio still on the loose with more guns with which to murder and leave Allison in his possession. No, I thought, we had no choice. This was the only way, and I knew Tom would feel the same. As for Pocko, he had made himself quite clear at the saloon.

Around one we crossed the river, the splashing water felt cool. On the other side we stopped for a short rest. There was tension among us, but we joked and made the best of the time we had left. We were extremely close now and within the hour would be at the stone bridge.

Grimes had mentioned meeting time as afternoon, not very specific, but helpful. If we were to arrive before Victorio, maybe we could make our move on just Granger and get out quick. Granger, I wanted bad, along with Allison, but of Victorio I wanted no part. Before leaving Kanab the thought of wiring Fort Apache' outside of Winslow crossed my mind, but I decided against it for what would hopefully turn out a good reason.

Just over forty minutes after remounting we were in sight of the stone bridge. Stopping a half mile from it, we hid the horses and continued on foot, each with a rifle in his hand.

There were cliffs all around us and we tried to stay on high ground. Back in Denver Tom had been a church-going man, and as I levered a round into the chamber, I told him… "If you have any connections left, now would be a good time to call in a big favor."

The sun had climbed high above us, and the heat caused us to sweat profusely, it streaked my face and the back of my shirt lay soaked between my shoulder blades.

If Victorio was there already he would have lookouts posted, and they would be watching for us. However, so far we had seen no one. Perhaps Grimes had lied after all. Maybe the meeting was going on right now, miles away, at some other location. If it was, then all was lost - including Allison.

The bridge grew larger as we moved closer, it was monstrous in size and the area beneath it certainly made for a perfect meeting point. Sweat rolled into my eyes and it stung. Wiping it out, I cursed to myself. Why weren't we seeing anyone? Where was Granger? Hell, where was Victorio? There was no denying my frustration. Steadily we moved along the ledge, crouched and ready.

Ahead of us over the arch, an Eagle flew into sight and soared in a slow gliding circle. He was watching something below… perhaps a prey, then again maybe a man, or men.

After twenty minutes of slow, careful climbing and maneuvering, we lay belly down on a high ridge just north of the bridge; it was a wondrous masterpiece, huge in size and we were so close we could have almost jumped onto it from where we lay. Beneath its giant arch sat Granger and his six men, smoking and talking within the shade beneath. Down from them fifty or so feet, was an unhitched wagon… probably loaded with guns. But best of all, tied to the front wheel was

Allison, and there was no Victorio. Apparently, he hadn't arrived yet. I wanted to yell out with joy.

Backing away from the edge of the ridge we sat and formulated a plan. There was no time to waste. To wait for dark would be nice, but by then Victorio would arrive. Granger would be expecting myself and Tom - but not a third gun, Pocko was our ace in the hole.

After throwing out several ideas, we came up with one we considered the best. Tom and I would climb down and approach the camp from the east and west. Pocko would remain in the high position and open fire from the ridge as soon as we were close enough to run in with our own rifles firing. That way, the only place they could maneuver was south - into a wall of rock.

The climb down took some time. With each passing minute I dreadfully anticipated Victorio's arrival, and with it the end to a good workable plan. The afternoon sky was rich with blue. The sun itself sat high behind Pocko and would serve as another advantage. Pocko would be able to see them clearly, but the glare looking up would be almost blinding.

There was no way of knowing for sure how Tom and I were doing as far as timing. A signal from Pocko would have been best, but to risky. So, it had been agreed that at 2:55 exactly, Pocko would start firing.

The climb to the bottom seemed like it would never end, and once again I was learning the meaning of patience. Timing was critical though and as I diligently descended; the jagged rocks tore at the skin on my hands. You could have wrung my shirt out for the sweat, but none of it mattered, for waiting below was Granger… and Allison Booker.

When I finally jumped down onto the ravine floor, I paused to look at my watch, 2:49. I had six minutes to move up the ravine and get in close without being seen. From the ridge above we had accounted for all of Granger's men. None had been posted as guards. Either he was overly confident or totally stupid.

Quickly and quietly, I moved toward the camp. The wagon was on Tom's side, and I hoped he could make it in close enough to cut Allison loose before the shooting started. The minutes ticked by as I moved forward. At 2:54 I was close as I dared to get without being seen. The men would be easy targets from here, and I was sure I could drop two or three before they realized what was happening.

With Winchester cocked I waited. The back side of the wagon was visible from my position, but I could not see the front half where Allison sat tied. Was Tom in place? I wondered if he had her cut free, or if he was even close enough to get to her once the shooting started. I looked at my watch, still 2:54. The second hand moved slowly - crawling its way toward the minute of truth… that moment Tom and I had been long awaiting - the final confrontation with Granger. Fifteen seconds left! I put away the watch and began a final countdown… 15 - 14 - 13 - 12… I hoped Tom was in position… 11 - 10 - 9 - 8… Pulling the Winchester to my shoulder, I bore down on the first man… 7 - 6- 5- 4- 3 - 2… NOW POCKO. The shot never came.

I swore under my breath. "SHIT." A few more seconds - it had to be the difference between our watches. PATIENCE. There was that damn word again. I was sure Tom was thinking the same thing. Seconds crawled by. "Come on, come on, damn it." I screamed in my mind for Pocko to fire, but he never did. Instead, he called out my name from the high ridge. His voice echoed across the silence, loud at first, but quickly fading away into the far distance.

I couldn't believe it, why in the hell would he do something so stupid? I looked up on the ridge where he now stood in plain view, the glare was nearly blinding, but through squinted eyes I could make out his form along with two warriors holding his arms. I felt a sudden sickness in the pit of my stomach, then Granger called out to me from behind the stone arch.

"Drop the rifle Steinberge. And the pistol too. Come in and join us. We've been expecting you." He called out to Tom and ordered him to do the same. The sickness in my stomach grew worse. I wanted to throw up, and I wanted to do it on Granger.

Dropping both rifle and gun belt, I walked in. Granger met me with a smile. Then Tom joined me at my side, and we stood together with five guns on us. Still tied to the wagon wheel Allison called to me, but Granger told her to shut up.

At the same instant sixty or seventy riders rode up the ravine toward us. They were Indians and out front was, Victorio.

The situation was Proof in what they say, "if it weren't for bad luck, I'd have no damn luck at all."

CHAPTER TWENTY-SIX

This had been an excellent trap, probably designed by Victorio… he was a smart one. No wonder the U.S. Calvary couldn't catch him.

When he and his men finally reached us, I saw that they had Pocko with them. The Mexican's hands were tied behind him and a lead rope had been placed around his neck - Victorio himself held the loose end. While the Chief and his warriors dismounted, Granger stepped in front of us.

When he spoke, his face was covered with a disgusting smile, and I was thinking how much better he would have looked with all his teeth missing.

"Well, Steinberge," he began, "it seems you didn't learn your lesson last time we stood face to face. I'll see if maybe I can't correct that this time. The next beating, I give you won't be so nice." He saw it in my eyes and warned me. "Go ahead, make a move, it'll be your last." His men stood ready, wanting me to make a play. Still grinning, his eye moved to Tom." And you, poor homeless man, all I can say is you had a fine wife. She was nice. Soft and sweet smelling. She never cried though, no matter what we did. She took it like a woman. I was the first and… Atop his horse Victorio yelled from behind Granger and there was authority in his voice.

"STOP what you do. You speak words that belong with the dirt beneath your feet. Even my warriors do not do such bad things as you have done. We kill, but only when it is the right thing, never for its pleasure. David Granger, you belong in the lodges with old women, not riding with men who know how to fight, live, and die bravely."

Granger's face turned red with anger, but he shut up quick. Even he had the brains to realize Victorio was no one to cross. Dropping the lead rope around Pocko's neck, Victorio dismounted and approached where we stood. Stopping beside Granger, he looked from me to Tom. "Which is the chief?"

"I am." I told him.

His eyes turned to me, and his face remaining sober. "You are the man called Steinberge?"

"Yes."

"Why have you come here, and how did you find us? Even your Army can not do this!"

"I have come for him." My eyes turned to Granger then back to Victorio. "He is wanted by my people for killing an innocent woman and her children." This time my eyes fell on Tom. "This is the man he wronged." Victorio looked into Tom Wade's eyes for what seemed a long time, then asked him. "This is so?"

Tom nodded. "Yes." His eyes came back to me, and he continued.

"Steinberge, I have heard of you. It is known that you once rode with the blue coats, scouting against the Indian people. Of this what do you say?"

"It is true I did." I told him, "But I was doing what I felt was the right thing."

Our eyes were locked. To look away would prove me a coward.

"How many Indians did you kill?"

"Many warriors, but only warriors, and I have suffered much at the hand of many Brave Chiefs such as yourself. There was Manuelito, chief of the Navajo, who even the great Indian fighter, Kit Carson could not catch. I was present during the great peace treaty with Chief Spotted Tail. In the Dakotas, I was one of many who fought against Sitting Bull and Chief Gall, and I carry a scar even now from the knife blade of Tall Bull of the Indian people. There have been others too."

"Did you ride with your General, Yellow Hair?"

"Custer! yes, but for only a season. I would not kill the Indian women and children as he ordered." I fell silent then, letting Victorio mull over what I had said.

The hot sun continued to blare down, but the giant arch of the Big Rock Bridge provided us shade and it felt good. I knew that if we had any chance at all getting out of this alive, it would be through Victorio. Like so many Indian Chiefs, he was a man of pride and held the tradition of honor with great importance. He looked at Tom once again for a long while then back at me.

"I will ask you once and search your eyes for truth."

"Have you used the white man's wire to tell the Army of this meeting?"

I shook my head. "No."

"Why have you not?"

"Because my fight is not with Victorio. It is with this man, Granger." I looked again at him then back to Victorio. "But I have not come just for him. I have also come for the woman I love – Allison Booker."

Both of our eyes turned to Allison and we stared for only a short time, then we were back looking at one another. He told me tartly.

"The woman is a gift to me from her brother Charles."

I wasn't sure where to go from here, but I figured I'd gone this far, what was there to lose, so I told him, "Charles Booker can no longer speak for her. He is dead."

"By your hand?" He asked.

"Yes, in a fair fight to which he challenged me." Victorio made a face, but I felt he believed me, so I went on.

"The woman Allison, I know, means a great deal to you. You find her of particular interest. But I love her and wish to make her my wife forever. We have already become one in love and know the true feelings that are now in our hearts. I will die for her."

Victorio turned then and looked at Granger. "You have heard?" Is this thing true? Is Charles Booker dead?"

Granger looked into my face. "I don't know. Maybe. I'd have to wire Tucson to know for sure. But if he is, I'll personally kill this son of a bitch."

Victorio frowned. "David Granger, you bring shame to me." Not pulling his eyes off Granger, he pointed a finger toward Tom," You take the life of this man's woman and his children, and it is alright. Steinberge kills your part brother in a fight that is fair, and you seek revenge on him. Even the children of my tribe have more understanding of what is fair and what is the truth." Shaking his head in disgust, Victorio continued. "Ride into the town on the other side of the river and speak across the wire. Find out if what this man has said is true… is Charles Booker dead? We will wait here for your return. If it has been a lie, he will die – they will all die."

While he was mounting, Victorio shouted after Granger. "And check if the little man Matt is there. He has never been late for our meetings."

Then Granger was gone, riding out with three of his men. The others remained I was sure to watch us… as if we were planning to go somewhere.

Victorio ordered the three of us tied to the wagon beside Allison, and for the time being that was fine with me.

The wagon itself stood alone in the bright sunlight, but tied to the wheels as we were, we were partially shaded. As soon as our hands were secured, and we were left alone I turned to Allison.

"I'm sorry about your brother." There was hurt in her eyes, but also a distant coldness.

"He's why I'm here. He GAVE me to Victorio. Arch, how could he do such a thing? He was my brother, flesh and blood. I mean, I know we never could see eye to eye, but to do this…" Her eyes grew wet, and she looked away. What could I say to her? This was one of those things that could only be worked out by her alone, within her own heart. I wanted to take her into my arms and hold her and I knew she would have liked that, but there were other things to worry about too - like how to get out of this thing alive.

Victorio would be the key. Not wiring the Army so far had paid off. I felt that even if I had sent them the information, there was no guarantee they could have possibly reached us in time. At least right now, Victorio would gain a little trust in us. To him that would mean a lot, yet then again, with men like him, you never know.

We sat through the afternoon tied to the wagon wheels. Victorio and his warriors slept or talked in bunches. Around four, Victorio himself and one of his men came to the wagon and checked its contents. It was full of new Army rifles, Springfield 45/70s, with ammunition and even official issue cartridge belts. Charles Booker certainly had power in the right places.

Satisfied with what he had seen, Victorio dismissed his man then walked around in front of us and stood a long while staring down. When he finally spoke, it was directed to Pocko.

"Why do you ride against me?" He asked.

Pocko spoke sternly. "I'm not here because of you, but because of the "shit" you are doing business with." Victorio smiled slightly then went serious again.

"Your face, David Granger did this to you?"

"Si."

"For what reason has he done this?"

"For pleasure."

Victorio folded his arms across his chest. "You wish to kill him then?"

Pocko nodded. "Si, with my bare hands."

"Looking to Pocko's right, he spoke to Tom.

"And you Tom Wade. Do you wish to kill him too?"

Tom thought before he spoke. "If Victorio harmed the mother and cubs of a great grizzly bear, what would the bear do to Victorio…? When my wife and children were murdered, there were others with Granger – they are all dead now, he is the only one left, and he was the one who led the others. Yeah, I want to kill him."

"And what of you Steinberge?" Moving in front of me, Victorio lowered himself to the ground and sat facing me.

"You are a man who serves justice to your people. You make sure your laws are kept and obeyed. Do you wish David Granger dead?"

Choosing my words carefully I knew what Victorio was thinking.

"Victorio," I began, "Had it not been for Tom Wade I would have died in the cold snows of Colorado. Sometimes my law does not see with good eyes. Perhaps their hearts are in the right place, they think that most men who are bad can be helped, but this is not always true. They have built jails and prisons for such men, but when freed, most of the bad one's harm again. I believe Granger is such a man. Only death could stop the harm he does."

Staring into my face a long while in silence, Victorio's eyes went to Allison.

"And of you… Allison Booker. How do you feel about your half-brother? Do you wish to see his life taken like the others?"

Allison gave her head a twist to clear the long hair from around her face. She did not get it all so Victorio reached out and swept it behind her shoulders. "Thank you," she told him, then went on. "Victorio, I'm sure that if Marshall Steinberge says he killed my brother Charles in a fight that was fair, then that is exactly what happened, and I believe my brother probably instigated it. He was my brother and I loved him, but Charles was a selfish man. To him, only money was important. He took what he wanted and right or wrong did not matter. My brother Charles was not a man of principles, and David Granger is no different, perhaps even worse. I don't wish him dead by the hand of any of these men, but I would like to see him put behind bars and left to rot."

Victorio studied her face. He was thinking over what she had said and weighing it; like the fact that she was a woman and considered weaker than a man, and too, how her beliefs stood up against his own- and I was sure he was looking at her the way a man does a beautiful woman.

*

Just at dark, Granger and his men returned. Riding into camp, they dismounted and talked with Victorio. Several minutes passed before they came down to where we were tied. Together they stood side by side looking down at us.

"David Granger tells me his brother is not dead, that he lives."

I felt everyone's eyes turn on me.

"Not so. I killed him myself."

"One of you does not speak the truth. Also, he says you cut the throat of Matt Grimes while he slept."

I remained calm, Victorio was watching me for the truth. It would be in my actions and in my eyes.

"Granger lies Victorio, and in so doing makes a fool of you… a Great Chief. He has harmed all of us and you are no different, he deceives you now."

Turning, Victorio called for two of his men to come to him. When they were there, he ordered Tom cut loose. As soon as he was free and, on his feet, Victorio walked away. "Bring him."

As they started after him, Granger began to follow too but Victorio stopped him. "No! You remain here." Then they were gone and out of sight.

Closing my eyes, I laid my head back against the wagon wheel. "Damn it," I thought. What can I do? I knew the answer, it was simple, – Nothing!

CHAPTER TWENTY-SEVEN

The sun was down when they returned with Tom. Eyeing him for damage, I sighed; there was none. Surprised, but thankful, I asked him how he was doing while they retied him to the wagon wheel. Victorio did not give him a change to answer me though.

"Your friend is well. We did not harm him. Only talk did we do, and he speaks what I think is truth. Of you I will ask to see if your words are the twin of his. I wish to know about your fight with Charles Booker and of the little man Matt Grimes, and too, I wish to hear what your heart speaks concerning the woman," he glanced at Allison then back at me. "The Mexican Army and the Army of your people is big and has many soldiers, but none of them, even with their learning in their schools, can catch me. But you, Steinberge, have done this. I am much surprised. You could have wired the soldiers but did not."

Victorio touched his heart with an open hand, continuing, "And here, in the heart that gives me life, I feel you are a man of truth and fairness. Like me, you fight for what you believe and will die for the same. If the big chief of your people was more like you or your friend Tom Wade, my people and your people would share this land, instead of covering it with our blood."

Victorio looked down at the ground in front of him for several seconds then back into my eyes saying, "Tonight, I will meet with my warriors, and we will talk of what to do with you. But I tell you, I am tired and though it is proud, my heart knows the end is near for us. Chief Joseph of the Nes Peirce will be remembered in your books for saying he will 'fight no more forever'. I too feel as he. But the whites keep taking from us what has been ours for seasons even beyond my Grandfather's Grandfather, we are treated as the animals of the forest, put on reservations like cattle behind your barbed wire holds. We are dying there, and our ways are being buried with our bones. Soon our young will not know who they are."

I saw wetness in his eyes. "Steinberge," he went on, "I ask you, what is wrong with the human being- that he could do such a thing to another?"

Behind Victorio the sun was slowly dropping out of sight, and though in our hearts there was anguish and grief, beyond us there was quiet and peace. Fires burned and Victorio's followers sat about talking. Mixed with them, Granger and his men boiled coffee and smoked, and above our heads in the heavens, stars were beginning to show themselves as a faded moon waited patiently for the sleepy sun to vanish.

Victorio watched me, looking into my eyes that he might glimpse the soul from which I was about to speak. What could I tell him? Looking up into the night sky I wondered if the color I saw was blue or black? Then back to Victorio I said.

"The question you ask has no answer. It is a great mystery. Why are there always wars and why do we take from one another? It seems for every question, there are more questions instead of answers. There are good people and bad people. Even if you believe there are good spirits and bad spirits. Maybe the bad spirits trick people and make them do wrong, and so long as there are bad people, the world will be as it is. To fix the world and give it peace, we must rid it of those who are bad." Victorio cut in.

"Does your government see my people as bad?"

"I do not know. At least I do not think so. In my world we have created an unstoppable beast that has two faces. One face is good and helps many, the other face is bad and hurts many. The creature of which I speak is called progress. My people thirst, perhaps wrongly, but thirst nevertheless, for improvement, better living. Unlike the Indians they cannot be satisfied or at peace with what they have. This creature I speak of spreads far and has much power. Perhaps it sees the Indians as its enemy. My heart is sick, because of what is happening to your people, but maybe your good spirits are looking after you in their own way."

The lines around Victorio's eyes widened as he waited to hear more. I could not help thinking that in his heart he was hoping my words would tell some final and magical solution. I could think of none but continued.

"Victorio, what my people are doing is wrong, but you cannot fight them and win. In years to come things will change, people will change. Right now, you must try and see the good working against the bad. I think the good spirits are doing that now. At least on the reservation, even if in secret, you can raise up your young in the old ways, the ways of your people. You can learn to write as us and put down on paper that which you wish to follow you. You are a proud people and always you will have your heart and your memories: the Mountains, the Streams and Lakes filled with fish, the Trees and even the Buffalo Herds that were once yours. You must believe your people will forever, through the stories, through love, and through the traditions you have lived by, will forever remain alive."

Victorio listened intently and the conversation continued for some time. I explained about Booker and Grimes and expressed my feelings toward Allison. How it stacked up against what Tom had to say, I had no way of knowing. At least Victorio gave no indication. Allison herself had told him she loved me and even at that Victorio gave no sign of what he was thinking.

When he rose and left to go gather his warriors, I followed him with my eyes. This man was not what the Army or newspapers had portrayed. Like us, he wanted peace too. It was just that to have it, he had to pay the entire price.

Just before they gathered for council, we were fed. Beyond that, the night was long and uninterrupted. The talks lasted till early morning and like us, Granger was not allowed to attend. Tom and I saw that as a good sign.

Throughout the night, Allison and Pocko catnapped- waking up for short periods, then dozing again. Tom and I talked. There would be no escaping from here. That our lives were solely in the hands of Victorio was not entirely true. His warriors would have a strong say. It was our feeling Victorio himself would put in a good word for us and give his personal recommendation…that would be our only hope.

The eastern sky was streaked with red across the horizon when Victorio came to us. There was light, yet it was still overshadowed by the dark of early morning.

His face sober, Victorio stood before us with arms folded. Granger joined him at his side and together our eyes stared up at them.

Like us, Granger was waiting to hear the word, except on his face there was arrogant confidence. His gun was low on his hip and near enough to grab if my hands would have been free. If I was to die, then die I would - my only wish was for Granger to go with me.

Then Victorio spoke, his voice authoritative against the semi-darkness around us.

"It has been decided. You, the man called Pocko." Victorio's face turned toward him, but I could not see his eyes. "You did not come here seeing me. You came for David Granger." His head shifted to Tom, "and you, Tom Wade. You too came for David Granger. As did you Steinberge, and you Allison Booker are also here, because of him."

Victorio's eyes swept across all of us as he continued.

"I do not wish to harm those who have no fight with me." Then turning he faced Granger. "You have heard. All these people are here because of you. You have brought pain and shame to them all. No longer will we do business. I think…" \

Victorio never finished his sentence. Granger drew his gun and held it on him. At the camp the warriors scrambled to their feet and waited. Granger's men were surprised, and, on their faces, I saw fear. Gun still pointed, granger tried to reason, knowing that what he had done was a gross error. But to try and back out now would be useless.

"Look Vic," Granger's voice was quivering, "we've been friends a long time. We've been doing business for a long time, right?" Victorio made no expression. Granger continued, "Nothing personal, but me and my men are riding out of here, that's all we want. You got the guns, so no hard feelings."

The warriors began to move, but Victorio stopped them by raising his hand.

Granger's fingers milked the butt of his pistol nervously.

"You try and stop me Vic, I swear I'll kill you. And just to be safe, I am taking Allison along. If you or Steinberge try to stop me, I'll kill her so neither of you can have her." It was fast and unanticipated. Tom's leg swung out in a wide arch and caught Granger's foot behind the heel. Down he came, slamming onto the hard rock floor, dead weight, but as he hit, his pistol discharged, the wild bullet tore into Tom's chest. His body bucked wildly against the wagon wheel and then went limp.

I screamed out his name and struggled against my bonds. Victorio's men were fast, they were on top of Granger and his crew in seconds.

Victorio ordered us cut free and I moved immediately to Tom's side. Blood was soaking into the front of his shirt. He was breathing, but it was shallow. Then suddenly, Allison was beside me and Pocko too, and together we gently laid Tom unto his back.

Slowly I rose…Tom's blood on my hands. Turning, I looked into Victorio's face. My voice was monotone and cold.

"Kill me now, this very minute, or allow me to face this man in a fair fight." Turning to face Granger who was being held by Victorio's warriors I said. "You and me mister. No men to hold me, no bullet in my head to slow me, and no one for you to call for help. No stopping until one of us is dead."

Victorio spoke out. "It will be as you wish Steinberge. You will fight come light, within a circle of my people. You will both fight till one of you has no more life."

*

Tom was taken into a Teepee to be left alone. There was nothing I could do for him except pray to the Maker, and even at that, I knew Tom's chance of making it were near impossible. I wanted to be by his side but was not permitted.

We were left untied, and as best we could, sat close, waiting for light of day. I sat with Allison in my arms. The loss of Tom was heavy in my heart and the relentless aching of hate-filled want – need - to meet Granger hand to hand kept me awake. In my restless mind I pondered how one single evil man could change the lives of so many in such a short period of time.

*

Warm morning light was everywhere when Victorio's men began gathering in a circle. The sun was bright. The shade of the Big Rock Bridge would be of no help against its glare since the circle was formed in the open space beyond the wagon. Beneath the circle of men was a floor of flat rock and the fight, which would soon be underway, could not be aided by any natural means. It would be man against man and muscle against muscle with the skill of the better fighter being the determining factor.

To Granger this fight was something he wanted too. He hated me and the authority I represented. To him, I was a threat to his lawless ways. His money had bought many other lawmen, thus opening the way for his wrong doings. But of me, there was no chance, only killing me could get me out of the way.

The day he had shot me, murder was the original plan, but luckily, I had angered him, and his pride got in the way. His motivation for winning was hate yes… but also vanity and egotism.

But now, the long-awaited time had come to me at last. I knew Tom would like to have been the one in the circle, but that couldn't be. This fight was mine now, and I would do it for both of us…for all of us.

Around ten, we were led side by side to the inner circle. Once there, we were ordered to remove our boots, socks and shirts. Facing one another at opposite sides, a knife was given to each of us. So, this would be it, a fight to the death with knives…Granger's favorite killing toy. Well, I wasn't a fat, ignorantly pompous businessman or small, frightened, little squeak of a human being. Nor was I a trusting, young, inexperienced deputy misled by a stolen badge. And that badge…I had noticed, was on the shirt Granger had removed and thrown down at his feet.

Around us the air hung motionless; we could feel the heat of it in each breath. I could already sense the Sun's burning rays on my back and chest, and the rock floor was noticeably warm against the bottoms of our feet. It was remarkably flat leveled, but with one drawback… there were tiny stones scattered sporadically within the circle.

Above us the sky was blue with clouds that seemed to be traveling faster than normal. The sun was bright, and I made a mental note to try and keep it to my back.

Victorio stepped into the inner circle and spoke to his warriors. "My people, you know what is expected. If one of these men tries to break from the circle, he is to be stopped and placed back into it. This is a fight to the death and only one can walk away. The spirits will help them fight and we will see if truth or untruth is stronger."

Looking at me then to Granger, Victorio said… "Let it begin."

From around us there arose a chant. It was loud and slowly Granger and I circled…ready, each filled of his own hate for the other. From the corner of my eye, I glimpsed Allison standing between Pocko and Victorio. Her face was white and strained, fearing the horror of the possible outcome.

Granger was grinning, liking the situation, happy that it was a battle of knives. He slashed out and I ducked letting it go over my head. He yelled with anger, "Shit." I swung my knife then and caught his shoulder, it opened and bled. Eyes locked, we moved carefully, continuing to circle, watching one another closely.

The sun was lifting higher and around us the stale heat increased, transforming the stone world in which we moved into an oven of rock. It baked our skin and sweat glistened our bodies, running down into our eyes in stinging streams. The chant was always present and added to the moment. Adrenaline flowed through our blood and pumped us full of energy that gathered in its momentum, working toward that final second of reckoning when death would finally come to one of us.

Granger slashed out and I moved back, then back in, trying for a cut of my own. Granger's eyes were full of shameless pleasure. I'd seen that look before, in men who had been overcome by the fear of battle and lost hold of the soundness and balance of sanity, slipping over the edge and loosing grip with reality, liking, thriving on the strange drawing power of killing another human being.

Granger lunged and somehow, we became locked in a clinch. His weight took me down and together we slammed hard onto the hot rock floor. I held the wrist holding the knife, realizing how stout Granger really was. Teeth gritted, I strained to hold off the shining blade, tip only inches from my throat. The chanting grew louder, and I could taste Granger's rasping breath. Then, above the chanting, I heard Allison scream my name and my knee came up, hard into Granger's groin. He grunted and rolled free of me. Scrambling to our feet, we circled once again. Our lungs burned from the heat and chests heaved from the torture of the dry heat. Victorio was right, I was the kind of man who would die for what he believed in, and right now killing Granger was the right thing. He jabbed twice with his knife then slashed out in a wild arch. The sharp blade caught the side of my neck, and I felt the burning sting of the cut. Flesh separated and blood surfaced, rolling down my chest. Feeling the wound with my hand I could tell it was deep, but it had sliced only the muscle and nothing vital.

Above our heads a bird flew over and for only a second its thin shadow crossed the circle. Faking a jab, I waited for Granger to move to block it then kicked at him with a tired leg. The kick was not on target, but it did cause him pain and he yelled out. Following with a swing of the knife, I sliced him across the chest. His scream was loud, and his running blood shined bright in the glaring sun.

Crouched and ready, we moved around each other with teeth that gritted against the pain we each felt. Minutes passed in sections of time that seemed endless and sweat seeped into our open cuts, increasing the pain and discomfort. Then it became a slash and a counter slash and for a fleeting time, a cut for a cut with red oozing; each adding to the feverish pitch of pain that screamed at our brain for relief.

Drenched in the crimson red of our own blood we moved with caution, our strength lessening. There was no referee, no one to interfere, no stopping. Every inch of my body screamed for me to quit and put an end to its' torture. Then somehow, we were clenched and falling.

We hit the rock floor with a hard thump, once again rolling over and over. Our muscles ached and in our temples raged a turbulent pounding. With the hand not holding the wrist with the killing blade, the other tried for a strike with a closed and sweaty fist. It became a maddening flurry of blow for a blow, each weaker than the last!

We were tired, void of energy, but there was no stopping. Not till death came to take one of us away. We were sweaty, blood covered bodies sliding like snakes on a blistering pit of stone. Only concentration coupled with dangerously weakening muscle held the arm with the deadly knife waiting to kill.

Chanting had become a distant mumbling in my ears as I focused all my remaining strength on Granger. It was coming to an end, and I knew that soon one of us would lay dead. My hand slipped from Granger's wrist, and I jerked my head to the side. His knife blade came down hard slicing my ear; its steel tip scraping the stone floor. For an instant he lost his balance. That was my chance!

With all the power I could muster, I thrust the glistening blade swiftly, sinking it to the handle deep into his side, he arched, then lowered his head and for only a second our eyes locked. He gave one final gasp of air, and it was over, he slumped lifeless on top of me.

I rolled him off and his body lay face up, sprawled on the hot rock floor. For a few seconds I laid staring at him, recalling all the harm he had caused. I looked at the knife sticking in his side, and under my breath I whispered, "That's for Tom."

Allison ran to my side, her eyes wet. Gently she nestled my head in her lap sniffling. Victorio kneeled beside me with a small piece of lead between his fingers. Placing it in my palm he said, "I think you would like this. My people dug it out of the wagon wheel behind Tom Wade. He smiled, Tom Wade has a clean wound, high through his right chest. I think he will be good as before." Touching my shoulder, he added. "You fight well Steinberge. It would be good if you were one my people. You would make a good Warrior." I smiled and thanked him for the compliment. Then looked into Allison's eyes and added, "I would be proud to fight beside you Victorio, but if you will allow it, I have other plans."

Victorio grinned wider, "Yes, I see. Now though my friend, it is time for my warriors, and I to go. We must keep moving to a place that is new, for soon the soldiers will come. They always find our old places," he winked, "But always too late."

*

Come dark only Allison, Tom and I remained. Pocko had given thanks then left for the ranch for which he worked. Granger's men had rode away taking with them his body. They would return it to the Booker Ranch for burial by order of the new ranch boss…Allison.

At supper I fed Tom broth with my old badge back on my shirt.

"You know," he told me with a smile, "It's about time you babysit with me for a while. Taking care of you was beginning to grow old, and while we're on the subject…Thanks for settling things." I winked at him. "My pleasure."

It was a beautiful night filled with a million stars. The fire flames snapped against a soft breeze and its light sent shadows dancing on the faces of the two most important people in my life.

Feeling good, I glanced up into the night sky thinking what a troubled time this Hunt had been. But now it was over. And here we sat peacefully outside of Kanob, Utah, beneath the beauty of the old Big Rock Bridge. A smile came to my face, and I told myself… 'you know Steinberge, this star-filled night is beautiful, so I here-by declare it a good omen, the start of a new beginning… for each of us.